Target Bella
Stay Frosty

A Few Good Men
Book Five

Jessika Klide Writing as
Stingray23

Author's Copyright

This is a work of fiction. Names, characters, organizations, places, events, and incidents are either products of the author's imagination or are used fictitiously. Any resemblance to actual events, locales, or persons living or dead are entirely coincidental.

Copyright © 2022 Stingray23 ALL RIGHTS RESERVED

No part of this book may be reproduced, or stored in a retrieval system, or transmitted in any form or by any means electronic, mechanical, photocopying, recording, or otherwise, without express written permission of the publisher.

This book is licensed for your personal enjoyment only. This book may not be re-sold or given away to other people.

Editing by: Maria Clark

Formatting by: Jessika Klide, LLC

Published in the United States of America

WHAT ARE OTHERS SAYING?

"Military men ... swoon-worthy spice, what's not to love?"

— *- USA TODAY* BESTSELLING AUTHOR XAVIER NEAL

"Adorable sexy ... just plain fun."

— -READ ALL ABOUT IT

"Hot ... enjoyable ... blissful ... loved every minute."

— -BOOK BANGERS BLOG

"Packed with so much action and heat."

— -WITHIN THE PAGES BOOK BLOG

Human Trafficking happens everywhere. To Men, Women, and Children of all Ages, Races, Nationalities, and Genders.

DONATE TO MAKE A DIFFERENCE: OURRESCUE.ORG

If you or someone you know is a victim of human trafficking, reach out for help or report a tip now.

National Human Trafficking Hotline
1-888-373-7888

Text "BEFREE" or "HELP" to **233733**

Email: help@humantraffickinghotline.org

National Center for Missing or Exploited Children
1-800-THE-LOST

Contents

The Navy Seal Creed   9

Chapter 1   17
Chapter 2   25
Chapter 3   31
Chapter 4   37
Chapter 5   43
Chapter 6   51
Chapter 7   61
Chapter 8   67
Chapter 9   73
Chapter 10   79
Chapter 11   85
Chapter 12   91
Chapter 13   97
Chapter 14   107
Chapter 15   115
Chapter 16   123
Chapter 17   129
Chapter 18   135
Chapter 19   141
Chapter 20   147
Epilogue   151

Jessika writing as Stingray23	183
Jessika writing as Cindee Bartholomew	185
Read Jessika's newest, sexiest, and most talked about bestsellers...	187
Stingray23	191
Stingray23.com	193

The Navy Seal Creed

In times of war or uncertainty there is a special breed of warrior ready to answer our Nation's call. A common man with uncommon desire to succeed.

Forged by adversity, he stands alongside America's finest special operations forces to serve his country, the American people, and protect their way of life.

I am that man.

My Trident is a symbol of honor and heritage. Bestowed upon me by the heroes that have gone before, it embodies the trust of those I have sworn to protect. By wearing the Trident, I accept the responsibility of my chosen profession and way of life. It is a privilege that I must earn every day.

My loyalty to Country and Team is beyond reproach. I humbly serve as a guardian to my fellow Americans always ready to defend those who are unable to defend themselves. I do not advertise the nature of my work, nor seek recognition for my actions. I voluntarily accept the inherent hazards of my profession, placing the welfare and security of others before my own.

I serve with honor on and off the battlefield. The ability to control my emotions and my actions, regardless of circumstance, sets me apart from other men.

Uncompromising integrity is my standard. My character and honor are steadfast. My word is my bond.

We expect to lead and be led. In the absence of orders, I will take charge, lead my teammates, and accomplish the mission. I lead by example in all situations.

I will never quit. I persevere and

thrive on adversity. My Nation expects me to be physically harder and mentally stronger than my enemies. If knocked down, I will get back up, every time. I will draw on every remaining ounce of strength to protect my teammates and to accomplish our mission. I am never out of the fight.

We demand discipline. We expect innovation. The lives of my teammates and the success of our mission depend on me — my technical skill, tactical proficiency, and attention to detail. My training is never complete.

We train for war and fight to win. I stand ready to bring the full spectrum of combat power to bear in order to achieve my mission and the goals established by my country. The execution of my duties will be swift and violent when required yet guided by the very principles that I serve to defend.

Brave men have fought and died building the proud tradition and feared reputation that I am bound to uphold.

In the worst of conditions, the legacy of my teammates steadies my resolve and silently guides my every deed.

I will not fail.

For the horses who help us heal.

Target Bella

ONE

Bella Rayne

YEARS AFTER I WENT INTO HIDING...

"HI, MICK," I SPEAK TO THE *SUDS AFTER BUD*/S bartender as I take a stool.

He walks up to me, "Hi, Bella Rayne. Your usual?"

"Yeah, make it a double, though," I tell him as

I look down the length of the bar to the small group of men playing billiards in the area just off the large dance floor. "I need it tonight."

"You got it." Mick acknowledges as he turns around, opens the cooler, reaches inside, and removes a chilled bottle of Crown Royal Regal Apple.

The group of studs yells in unison in triumph, drawing my attention back to them. One of them pretends to be shot as another holds his pool stick over his head, announcing, "FNG buys the next round, boys!"

I smile and ask Mick as he pushes my frosted low-ball glass full of ice and golden-colored alcohol across the bar to me. "FNG?"

"Fucking new guy," he explains.

I laugh at the acronym, then look back at the studs. "SEALs?"

"Affirmative. They're just back from a deployment."

I lift my glass and sip the soothing ice-cold liquor. "He looks too young to be a SEAL."

Mick chuckles, "Bella Rayne; I'll let you in on a little secret. The older you get, the younger everyone else looks."

"Apparently!" I laugh and lift my glass in a

salute to his wisdom. Then I glance over and study the eye-candy antics as I enjoy my drink. The group of heroes appears to be in their late twenties to early thirties, my age. The only one who doesn't is the FNG.

I smirk at Mick, "Well, I trust he's at least twenty-one...."

He nods.

As I turn to watch them blatantly, I ponder. "Oh, to be twenty-one again."

Mick rejects my wistfulness, "No, thanks! No do-overs for me."

"Really? Come on. Do you mean to say you wouldn't want a redo? Wouldn't you change anything? Do things differently?"

He chuckles at my disbelief. "I didn't say that."

I laugh and spin my glass on the bar mixing the melting ice with the hard liquor. The cubes tinkle against the glass. "I would. I would swear off men altogether and focus solely on my career."

"Bad man, eh?" His eyebrow cocks knowingly.

"Pure evil, Mick." I nod, then shiver. I haven't thought about my abusive past in years.

My former lover, my ex, my number one mistake that cost me my dreams, Manny Morales, wore a three-piece suit like no one else, commanded a room when he walked in, and flashed cash as it came into his possession too quickly. I was fresh out of high school with no hope of affording college, and foster parents who though they loved me, needed my room for the next needy homeless child. I was officially an adult and ripe for the grooming, which Manny did with such skill and finesse that I was completely fooled.

I thought he was an extraordinarily successful young entrepreneur, but it turned out his uncle ran a Mexican cartel. I shiver again and drain my glass, remembering when I accidentally discovered those pictures of the girls bound and beaten on his phone and realized his business was sex trafficking. They were victims who tried to escape. It was like a veil fell away, and I saw him clearly as the devil he is.

He wasn't supposed to return from his business trip to Mexico until after the weekend, so I was surprised when I unlocked the door and found a strange set of keys in the bowl on my foyer table. I hadn't seen a familiar car in the parking lot, but he had an endless supply of different vehicles.

When I entered my bedroom, it was empty. The shower was running. He wasn't expecting me to come home early, or his phone and wallet wouldn't have been tossed carelessly on top of his clothes, lying on my bed.

It lit up with a message; of course, I was curious. He was secretive about his business affairs and guarded his phone. I seized the opportunity to spy on him. I picked it up and read the text. It was in Spanish.

Jefa, putas capturadas y castigadas.

Which translates: "Boss, whores caught and punished." Then a picture came through. The blood drained from my face, and vomit entered my mouth.

Three girls, younger than me, wore metal collars around their necks and were chained together. They were naked, dirty, battered, and bloody. I dropped the phone and took a step back.

Shock turned to terror.

I grabbed my backpack and threw it out of the room toward the front door. Then I grabbed Manny's stuff and ran into the kitchen. I took nearly $10,000 of cash out and stuffed it in my bra. Then I put his phone on top of a burner on the stove, piled his clothes on top, and turned on all of them.

I raced back to the bedroom and locked and closed the door to keep the smoke from reaching him.

Then I grabbed our keys, slung my backpack over my shoulder, and hurried out. No one was outside. I bolted the door behind me and clicked his key fob to find out which was his car. The car parked next to mine unlocked.

I ran to my car, opened my door, and tossed his keys in. I set my backpack on the driver's seat, unzipped the pocket holding my survivors' knife, and stabbed his car's front and rear tires to flatten them. I returned the blade to its holder. Then shoved my backpack out of the way, climbed behind the wheel, and fled the scene.

I turned east out of my parking lot and called my foster brother, Enrique, who worked at the Yellow Rose Equine Therapy Ranch, and asked him to saddle my mustang, Smokey.

When I crossed the river bridge, I tossed my phone and Manny's keys out the window. Then drove to the truck stop and parked my car. I went into the bathroom, changed my clothes, and came out a cowgirl.

I hitched a ride with a trucker to the west side of town and walked the rest of the way to the ranch. When I arrived, Enrique and a saddled Smokey were waiting.

He took one look at me and said, "Don't tell me. I don't want to know. But good luck." Then he hugged my neck, and I rode off into the sunset.

Smokey is the only reason I'm alive today. He saved my life twice. The first time from falling into a deep, dangerous depression when I lost my family and entered foster care, and the second time, being my untraceable ride out of Texas.

I later changed my name from Allison Girard to Bella Rayne Parker. Eventually, Smokey and I ended up in San Diego and settled down. I figured the West Coast home of the Navy SEALs would be a safe place to establish a new identity. I went to nursing school and love my work in the hospital's trauma unit.

I ask Mick, shifting the focus of the conversation away from me. "What would you do differently?"

"I would realize I wasn't bulletproof." He

smirks, then winks. "At twenty-one, I thought I was."

I frown. "You've been shot?"

"In the line of duty. I'm former law enforcement." He nods.

"A cop?"

He smirks, "Secret service."

"Oh wow! That's cool!"

"What are you doing bartending then?"

He grins, "working for tips."

The group of SEALs at the billiard table yells again, and Mick tosses his head in their direction. "Those guys are the only bulletproof men in the world."

Then he looks down the bar at a man holding an empty glass and tells me, "I'll bring you another after I take care of him." He turns away and walks down to the needy customer.

Two

Bella Rayne

I LOOK AROUND THE BAR. IT'S MONDAY NIGHT and slow. I've been coming here to unwind for the past few months. Working at the Trauma Center of the hospital takes its toll on the psyche. There is only so much pain and suffering you can see daily without some escape from reality.

Since *Suds After BUD/S* bar is famous as a haunt for SEALs, it's the only place I feel safe to go alone to have a drink before heading home to my empty apartment. The owner, Jeff Crockett, is a local legend, a former Navy SEAL; rumor has it, his side hustle is a security company that combats human traffickers.

The young SEAL walks to the bar and stands next to me, waiting for Mick to take his order. I give him a quick up and down, enjoying the shredded, hard physique of youth and his nice ass. His body is a pure athlete without an ounce of fat. I bet he's agile, quick as a cat, and can fuck forever.

My eyes travel up to his face. He is cute. Like ... really cute! The cocky smirk he wears is a permanent expression, and it shouts, I guarantee a good time and a satisfied smile afterward hit me up for a quick fuck.

I grin at my glass before I take another sip, letting the alcohol coat my pain. I close my eyes and enjoy the burn. If I was ten years younger.... Hell, I would take him up on that open invitation if I were five years younger. But thirty-two is a long way away from.... I twist my seat to get a better view and size up his age. He can't be older than twenty-one.

I lift my glass to my lips and stare at him,

wondering why he joined the military instead of attending college on some sports scholarship.

His face tilts slightly upward, and I realize he's aware I'm sizing him up, and he's intentionally ignoring my brazenness. I take another sip and finally begin to feel the effects of the amber liquid.

I smirk at his profile, enjoying that our age difference has advantages. I can gawk unheeded and even drool without him hitting on me with my older sister vibe.

I drain my glass and set it on the bar without taking my eyes off him, and he glances down. Our eyes connect, and I see the cutest damn twinkle in his.

He's fucking cocky. I wonder how hard the SEAL instructors were on him. I'm sure their goal was to wipe that smug look off his handsome-as-hell face forever, but they failed. They so failed.

He takes the stool next to me, but instead of politely facing forward, he swings his legs, hooking my knee and pushing mine apart. Spreading them so adeptly, I'm shocked to find him sitting intimately inside them. It is a slick as hell aggressive move, totaling catching me with my guard down. He isn't looking at me as a big sister but as a cougar that he's more than willing to accommodate.

A deep rush of desire floods my body. *Oh, man, am I ever horny.* He leans forward, and pure seduction seethes from him. *Fuck, he smells good.* His masculine essence oozes into my safe zone, and when his soft voice barely above a whisper says, "Whoever turned your sunshine blue needs to have their ass handed to them." His deep voice is sexy as fuck, and I detect a very slight Texas drawl.

A quick flash of him as a bare-chested Cowboy in a hat and boots wearing chaps sends shivers straight to my clit, and as I stare into his daring green eyes, my pussy saturates my panties. This bad boy is a badass. He isn't boasting. He's brazen about the fact.

I swallow the spit that floods my mouth. I'm too old for him, but his aggression mixes dangerously with the anguish of losing a young life today and the effect of drinking alcohol too quickly on an empty stomach. I can't stop myself from flirting, "You offering?"

He chuckles, and the smirk deepens to a grin with two cute dimples, "I am." He boasts, and his eyes drip sex. "Point him out, and I'll take him out. Or I can make your sun shine so radiantly that one look at you, and his ass will be handed to him on a silver fucking platter."

DAMN! My pussy draws up tight with want and need, believing every word.

Mick steps up to the bar and pushes my second double to me, attempting to break the spell. "How many drinks are you buying, young padawan?"

The FNG gives me a wink before he reluctantly looks away and corrects Mick. "That's Jedi, and a round of beer for Alpha on me."

Mick lets the reproach roll off his back. Probably, not wanting to damage the size of his tip. He nods, turns to the cooler, and begins removing Budweisers, placing them on the bar. The group of five studs comes over, and each takes one. The FNG gives them his attention but doesn't relinquish his dominant position between my legs, and I can't help feeling flattered.

Staring at his facial expressions as he good-heartedly absorbs the jabs and teasing they give him, he holds his own with them as equals. He takes the last beer remaining and salutes them, holding it up.

Then he turns his intense focus back on me. I melt with the implied compliment that this young buck is totally into me. Trying to convince myself he's too young that I shouldn't is pointless. It doesn't feel wrong. It feels very right.

Three

Jayden

I reach out, grinning at her, and tap her shoulder, "Excuse me, Miss."

Her brows furrow, confused as to why I did that. But she doesn't realize I'm making sure everyone else knows she's mine.

No sooner has the words left my lips than Aiden Braswell takes the cue and removes my hand, telling me, "Hey, hey, now." Then tells her, "Not to worry. We got this."

Immediately, the team encircles us, and I belt out the first lines to "Lost That Lovin' Feelin'," and we reenact a serious rendition of the bar scene straight out of the movie *Top Gun*.

She rolls her eyes and laughs hard at us; the beauty radiating from her smile is pure gorgeousness. Then she nods her head and says, "Okay, okay, he can stay."

As the song winds down, Mick serves up another round of beer, knowing that cost me again. The team takes fresh bottles back to the pool table as I devour my cougar with my eyes.

When we are alone again, I introduce myself with my sideways grin that shows off my dimple and my killer wink that always seals the deal. "Jayden 'Jedi' Evans, I am."

She laughs easily again and offers her hand for me to shake. "Bella Rayne Parker."

As I slide my hand over hers, I practically moan her name, "Bella Rayne...." Then I squeeze it firmly and pump it with a distinct rhythm, "That's a beautiful name."

The surge of desire that shoots through me is exactly what I expected from her. She's older, mature, respectful, fun-loving, and lonely. A woman who won't demand anything more from me than a good fucking which I am looking forward to giving her.

She bites her bottom lip, and I realize she isn't a Frog Hog. She's here to unwind. Staring intently at her, running different scenarios about why she chose *Suds After BUD/S bar*, she unravels under my gaze and answers with a breathy, "Thanks."

Triumph mixes with desire when I recognize I'm winning her submission.

"So, you come here often," I state the fact.

Her eyebrow cocks, and a trace of suspicion hangs in her words. "Why would you assume that?"

I smirk as I shake my head. "No reason other than when you walked in, Mick knew you."

Her expression relaxes, and she teases me. "Have you been watching me the whole time?"

I grin my sideways grin again, "Busted."

She smiles, pleased with my confession. "Very astute observation, young Jedi." Then she tells me, "Yes, I come here often to unwind."

I hold up my beer bottle and say, "Here's to unwinding together." I can feel my eyes dancing with desire as I look her curvy body over and make a plan to nibble and suck her parts until she screams my name.

She lifts her glass to my toast, "We shall see."

I laugh, "Indeed. We shall."

Then I take a nice long confident draw on the bottle, and her eyes hone on my Adam's apple as it moves up and down as I swallow.

She reaches for her glass and takes a big gulp of what I can only guess is cougar courage. She's obviously not accustomed to picking up strangers.

"FNG! Yo! Get your young, inexperienced ass over here. We're thirsty again. It's time to lose another game and buy another round."

I tip my head and chuckle, then lift my face to stare into her eyes. I want her to know I'd rather stay where I am. That I'm not finished with her, and I want her to stay put, to wait for me, but I won't ask her to.

I see the want to in her eyes, and her face flushes with desire. I drop my eyes to her breasts, and her nipples are hard with need.

The urge to kiss her washes over me and I look at her parted lips. But now is not the time. I lick mine and give her a wink that promises I will return to finish what I started with her.

Standing, I shake my head, open my hands, and jab Aiden. "Can't you see I'm busy here, bro?"

Everyone laughs before he answers, "Don't embarrass us, young Jedi. She is out of your league."

"Says who?" I give him a cocky head nod as I swagger away from Bella Rayne.

Aiden beacons me, taunting, "When you can snatch a victory from the pool gods, you will be dismissed to pursue the Frog Hog. But not before, young Jedi."

Four

Bella Rayne

I turn back to the bar and hover over my drink. Listening to the men's playful banter as the clicks reverberate when the cue ball strikes the other billiard balls, sending them rolling across the table while country music mingles with their voices.

As soon as Mick comes back over and wipes the bar with a damp cloth in front of me, I ask him for clarification. "Frog Hog?"

"SEAL ho." He states without judgment.

"Oh!" I blush at having been labeled a prostitute.

He chuckles, "Don't take it the wrong way. The term is not a criticism. It's a fact of their lives. A consequence of being the baddest asses on the planet. They have their groupies, just like rock stars."

"Oh! I get it." I smirk at my drink, "Like Rodeo Buckle Bunnies." I look down the bar and realize I'm the only woman here. "Is it safe to assume the bar is full of Frog Hog's on the weekend?"

He grins, "It is." Then he tosses his head and says, "If you're looking for something to take the edge off other than liquor, I hear hooking up for a one-night-stand with a Navy SEAL is the ticket."

I laugh, "So, you're pimping for them?"

He chuckles, "No. Trust me. They don't need my help. But you admitted you come here to unwind because they are here, and you feel safe. Just letting you know the word at the bar among their groupies. There are other benefits to consider on the table as well."

I look over at the pool table. Jayden's eyes are

on me and not the game. He looks like he wants to devour me, and my pussy throbs.

Mick chuckles again. "The young Jedi is serious."

I laugh and push my glass at him. "I better have another then, you know, 'cause of the age gap."

He takes my glass and says, "This one's on me."

I look over my shoulder to see Aiden lifting the triangular rack off the billiard balls and Jayden bending over the table to strike the cue ball. My mouth waters as his head goes down and his straight legs, muscular thighs, small waist, and tight ass cheeks are on full display.

Just then, a man in his forties blocks my view as he steps up to take the stool Jayden vacated. "Mind if I sit down?" Without waiting for my answer, he sits.

I look back to see Jayden grinning and giving banter back as good as he's getting, then he bends back down and aims. Watching his big arm flex as he pulls the cue stick back, sliding it smoothly over his fingers resting on the table as his guide sends my tongue out to lick my lips.

Then he jabs the cue ball, sending it with

force into the racked set, busting the balls with a loud, sharp crack of sound. As he stands upright, admiring his skill, he glances at me. His head rises as his shoulders square, and his chest puffs slightly when he sees the dude sitting on his stool.

I smirk at the unsuspecting man with his tattooed forearms leaning on the bar, trying to get Mick's attention.

Then I turn around to watch Jayden, leaning my back on the bar. He's wiggling the blue chalk cube on the tip of his stick as he examines the layout of the balls across the table. Then he walks around the table, chooses his target, calculates the angle, and determines the amount of force necessary to not only sink the target but maneuver the cue ball to set up the next one. I watch, fascinated with his split focus and quick decisions as he moves around the table. As soon as he sinks the shot, he looks over at me. Then he proceeds to aim the next ball.

The SEALs harass him as well as each other, using words like sandbagging, hustler, and pool shark.

"Do I know you from somewhere?" The man next to me asks.

"No," I answer without hesitation, smiling at Jayden, who is making short work of winning the billiard game now that someone else is sitting next to me.

"Are you sure?" He insists he recognizes me. "I never forget a face."

I shake my head, "I don't either, and I don't know you."

"Hmm," he says, "My name is Paulo."

I nod but don't offer mine.

"And you are?" He pushes.

"None of your business."

Just then, Mick returns with my double shot of Crown Apple, and I take it, thanking him, then turn back to watch Jayden sink the eight ball to win the game. While Paulo places his order for a top-shelf tequila shot, the eight ball drops, and the SEALs shout, "HOOYAH!"

Instantly, the other SEALs throughout the bar echo the cry, "HOOYAH!"

Paulo flinches, looking around, uncomfortable. As if he wasn't aware he was in a bar full of Navy SEALs.

Jayden turns his cute boyish grin on me as he's slapped on the back and congratulated by his teammates.

As Jayden and his team make their way back to the bar to claim the round of beer that Mick has placed on the counter, I'm aware he's set Paulo's shot of tequila down as well.

Paulo slides his money to Mick, slams the shot back, and says as he turns to leave before the SEALs arrive, "Nice to meet you...?"

"Yep" is my distracted response.

FIVE

Jayden

SMART MOVE, BUDDY. I THINK TO MYSELF AS I watch the dude vacate the barstool next to Bella Rayne.

As soon as I arrive, I slide onto it, take a beer, and bring the bottle to my lips to drink half of it, calming my jealous reaction to seeing someone else hitting on her. I hadn't intended to show my teammates my billiard skills this early. My goal was to lose a few games to string them along later for some quick cash.

But this beautiful woman with her soft brunette hair, dark brows and lashes framing clear blue eyes, and a freckled nose that indicates she grew up outside in the sun, has already gotten under my skin like an itch that needs to be scratched.

She doesn't say anything, nor do I until we are alone. Then I turn to her and ask, "Want to dance?"

She looks surprised but nods, "Sure." She takes a sip of her drink, then sets it on the bar.

I stand, hold my hand out for hers, and she slips hers inside. The intense desire I felt the first time I touched her returns, and my cock thumps.

She doesn't resist or stiffen when I draw her into my arms. She is relaxed and at ease with my dominant personality. I chalk it up to her being older and more mature. Unlike girls my age, who feel threatened by me just being me, and who don't get the commitment required to be a SEAL, nor the sacrifice, I make for my country serving as a special warfare operator.

As we sway to the music, getting acquainted,

I ask her. "You aren't from San Diego, so where are you from?"

She stiffens, flinching, and I'm surprised to feel her fear. Trying to put her at ease, I blab, "I grew up in Houston, Texas."

"Really?" She says, deflecting, "Don't people from Texas have a distinct drawl?"

I chuckle, "First order of self-improvement when I was accepted as a candidate to become a SEAL was to shed my hometown enunciation. I figured it would be one less thing that made me an easy target during BUD/S."

"Good thinking." She laughs, "I can only imagine how hard they tried to conquer that smirk of yours, though."

It appears for her, as I admit, "Very. They tried very hard."

"I'm glad they didn't succeed," she says, looking up at me from under her gorgeous long eyelashes, and my cock thumps again. Then she says, "I'm from Texas as well. Small world, isn't it?"

"Yes, it is," I pull her closer to me. "You've lost your drawl too."

"Mmhmm," she doesn't explain, so I assume she's been gone from there long enough to lose it.

Guessing from her curves, she's probably in her early thirties.

As we sway to the music, she fills up my senses, dominating me, and it's the damnedest thing. I don't want to let her go, but the slow music stops. Breaking apart with the faster beat of the next song, her moves are sensual and fluid, not jerky, so I move up on her, and she grooves against me.

The promise of an evening tangled with her in the sheets is becoming more and more plausible.

After we've danced to several songs, she takes my hand and leads me back to the bar. We finish off our drinks, and Mick brings us another round.

"This round is courtesy of Alpha." He winks at me and grins at Bella Rayne. I look around for my teammates to thank them, but no one is left.

Mick chuckles, "Let me know if you need an Uber." Then he walks away.

Bella Rayne lifts her drink to her lips, takes a sip, and I down the first third of my beer; then, she addresses the elephant standing between us. "How old are you, Jayden?"

"Old enough," I tease her.

"How old is old enough?" She cuts her blue eyes at me.

"Old enough to know age is just a number." I take another hit on my beer, then set it down.

She blows a puff of air out of her full lips, "That's what people say when they don't want to face the truth and are trying to hide from the reality that it's a bigger number for some of us than others of us."

I chuckle, then turn to face her, capturing her legs between mine like before. I reach up and move a stray strand of hair off her cheek, pushing the length over her shoulder to fall down her back. Then I place my finger under her chin, tilt her beautiful face to look squarely into mine, and stare into her unsure age-gap guilty eyes.

"I disagree. That's what people say when they don't let the limitations of an arbitrary number interfere with living the life they choose to live."

She blinks, absorbing my meaning.

"If I had listened to your interpretation, I wouldn't be a member of Alpha right now."

Her eyes search mine, and I stare her down.

"Why should age factor into any equation? If you let other people set your parameters, you limit yourself to what they say you can do."

I lean in closer and whisper. "Set yourself free, Bella Rayne. Your life is yours to live how you choose to. The heart wants what the heart wants."

I let her chin go and back away. "Unless you're using it as a lame-ass excuse to tell me to fuck off."

Her expression is exactly what I hoped for. She doesn't see me as a young man now. She sees me only as a man.

I cup her face with my hand and continue to convince her as I close the gap between us. Proving my point in a way words can never win the argument for or against age making a difference over what the heart wants.

Right before I touch my lips to hers, her breath pauses in her chest. I give her a moment to experience the choice my heart made the moment I saw her walk into the bar. When Mick recognized her and talked to her like a regular, I knew she would be my next conquest, and from the chaos roaring through my body right now, quite possibly my last.

There was something different about her that stirred something different inside me.

Never backing down from a fight or a

challenge, I kiss her.

Her mouth is succulent. The shape of it fits perfectly. Her taste is luscious. Her kiss is nothing like any other woman's. As I slip my tongue inside her mouth, my abs harden, constricting, pulling my balls up tight, and my cock floods with blood, lengthening with a full erection within seconds.

Goddamn. She is fucking delicious!

At first, she is passive, letting me explore her. But when I crush her body against mine, and she feels my hard cock pressing against her softness, all pretense of a demure older woman vanishes. She melds herself against me, sucking my tongue down her throat and moaning like the whore she wants to be for me.

I let her mouth go, and I lead her out of the bar without asking. I hesitate between taking her into the stairwell to bang right now or the elevator to escape with her for the entire night.

I choose the elevator, knowing she is more than a quick fuck. But she overrides me, pulling me into the stairwell. When the door slams shut behind us, she is in my arms, pulling my mouth to hers, and I back her up against the wall, pinning her there, then proceed to devour her.

Six

Bella Rayne

Dear God! Jayden is aggressive, confident, and fearless. His body is perfection. His skin is warm, soft, firm, and beautiful. His scent is clean, fresh, masculine musk. Everything about this man turns me on.

Until now, no one has created a want and need overwhelming everything else. I melt under his onslaught.

Yes! Yes! Yes! My mind screams as my hands

slide around his neck, hooking him to me. His hand presses the small of my back, crushing me against him. We kiss like we are drowning, and the other is our oxygen.

It's been over a decade since Manny's betrayal. I've dated, but by the third date, I'm done. I can't get past the trust issue enough to let go.

I'm not sure what the hell has happened with Jayden, but in the span of a couple of hours, he's pole vaulted over the barrier I erected to protect my freedom.

Maybe the catalyst was his whispered words, "Set yourself free, Bella Rayne. Your life is yours to live how you choose to. The heart wants what the heart wants."

Maybe it's the way my body tuned into his. Like there is an unknown magnetic force drawing me to him.

Maybe it's purely chemical, like two drugs combining to make a cure.

Whatever it was, I want this young stud to fuck me senseless.

One of his big hands pushes under the waistband of my pants to cup my ass. As his lips leave my mouth and travel down my neck, kissing and nipping tiny bites of my fevered flesh, he pinches the clasp of my bra, releasing my tits from their confinement. At the same time, the other slips inside my shirt under my bra to tease my taut ripe nipple.

My eyes roll back in my head as it lolls against the wall with the exquisite sensations of his seduction. Then he slowly lowers his body to squat before me, pushing my pants down as he goes, pinching my nipple, distracting any coherent thoughts.

Suddenly, he yanks, and my pants fall to my ankles, binding me in place. Before I panic, I feel the cool air hit my exposed pussy.

"Mmm," he moans.

A tsunami wave of desire surges through my veins, and my knees buckle. My pussy drowns itself. My clit hardens and protrudes from its protective hood of skin.

He lifts my left foot as deftly as a farrier lifts a horse's hoof and frees my high heel from the fabric. Then his mouth is branding me with burning kisses and nibbling nips. He's done this countless times.

My clit begs for his attention. My pussy

throbs for his dominance. I don't care that I'm joining the ranks.

He spreads my legs apart, setting my foot down wider than before. His hot kisses and his caressing hands travel up, tickling the tiny white hair along my sensitive inner thighs, making his way to my paradise.

I push my legs apart for him as a moan heavy with anticipation escapes my mouth.

My hands latch into his hair when his tongue swirls my clit. As he licks and sucks, my moans echo in the stairwell.

When my legs begin to quiver, trembling, and on the verge of orgasm, I start to cry. Biting my tongue to stop my sobs, I accept Jayden's affection as genuine. No strings attached. No manipulation. Just mind-blowing sex, the way it is meant to be enjoyed. I breathe his name, "Jayden," freeing myself from the scars of sexual abuse.

"Mmmm," his moan sounds like a growl as all 6'2" of physical perfection stands. His cocky smirk hovers over me as he unzips his pants and pulls out a big, beautiful cock. Then this honorable man asks, "You good with this?"

My heart leaps into my throat as my soul

sings. "Yes, Jayden 'Jedi' Evans, I am so good with this."

And with that, Jayden's mouth seals my trauma in my mouth, and his tongue thrusts it down my throat as his gorgeous cock sinks inside me and pounds all memories of another age, another place, and another man.

There is only Jayden, and I moan his name repeatedly as he hammers five explosive orgasms out of me.

Finishing, banging my body against the wall, he cups my face between his hands, stares into my eyes, and overrides everyone ... forever.

Then he's wrapping his arms around me, pulling me tight to his body, and reversing our position so he can lean against the wall and rest. I unwrap my legs, lay my cheek on his chest, and listen to his lionheart thump.

He balls his fist in my hair and pulls my head back. He stares into my captured eyes and tucks his cock back inside his pants. He tenderly kisses my lips when he deftly hooks my bra back together.

He lifts me like I weigh nothing, changing positions with me again, and squats down. While I tuck my tits away, he removes my high heel, places my foot carefully through my pants leg, then puts my shoe back on.

When he attempts to pull my pants up, I tell him, "I got it from here."

He stands, grinning, then retreats far enough away I can wiggle back into them. Then he holds out his hand, and I slip mine inside.

As we make our way down the stairs to the lobby, he says, "I'm sorry you've been hurt before. Whatever happened to you is in the past. Lock it away and throw away the key. Rehashing it and trying to make sense of it won't change it. It will only rob you of more of your precious time."

I cut my eyes at him. Amazed that he noticed, but even more amazed that he would say something. He wasn't condescending. He was being genuine. "Is that some sort of SEAL wisdom?"

He shrugs and pulls open the stairwell door. "Jedi advice."

I pause for a second, then smile at him as I walk through.

"SEAL advice would go something like, 'Suck it up, buttercup. You survived. Now, thrive.'"

I laugh and tell him, "I'm a trauma nurse at the hospital. Can I quote you on that?"

"Absolutely."

Grinning, I pause, watching the people coming and going, and when he joins me, I ask. "Will I see you again?"

"Sure. I'll be hanging out here with my brothers." He puts his arm around me, and we make our way to the parking lot. I slip mine around his waist, and our strides sync.

Remembering what Mick said about the bar being full of Frog Hog's on the weekends, I clarify. "I want to see you again."

"Do you?" He asks, amused at my temerity.

"I do," I answer truthfully. There is something about him that makes me happy, and if I've learned anything helping people who are fighting for their lives, it is that life is too short. I haven't had a lot of happiness in my life, and I like the smile he's put on my face. It feels good. Why not? Why shouldn't I feel good? Why can't I live my life happy? "I've had a really good time tonight."

"I can see that." His cocky smirk returns as he looks down at me. "Your sun is shining more radiantly than when you walked in the bar for sure."

"Mission accomplished," I laugh but then

speak sincerely. "Listen, don't get me wrong. I'm not talking about a full-fledged romantic relationship with commitment and expectations. I'm just looking for a casual friend with some amazing skills to destress with. I had a rough day at work and hooking up with you.... Well, sex is better than alcohol at handling it. Both of our careers are highly stressful and .... You know, the age-gap thing could work to our benefit. I'm too old for you, and you're two young for me, but the sex was incredible."

He doesn't say anything. He hesitates.

Shit! He's not that into me!

"But if you're a one-and-done dude, I respect that. I thoroughly enjoyed my one you have done." I wink and pretend I'm totally cool with his rejection. But inside, I'm crushed. I don't meet people easily, and I don't hook up casually. He's the astronomical exception.

"One and done?" He chuckles. "I counted four. Possibly, five."

I'm too damn old for the blush that creeps into my face. Yet, there it is. I drop my eyes, unable to bear the embarrassment.

He stops and pushes a stray hair behind my ear, exposing my expression. Then he calmly asks, "What would you say to being *my* Frog Hog?"

Surprised at his using the term, mixes with relief that he's into me enough to want to hook up again. I lift my eyes to his. "Your Frog Hog?"

"Yeah, my on-call, go-to fuck?" He grins, "We'll stay frosty with each other. No commitment ... no strings ... just balls to the wall —banging."

Now, I hesitate, absorbing his words.

His cute as fuck dimples tease me. "Isn't that what you just described?"

I nod, realizing he's agreed to my terms. "Sounds perfect."

"My place tonight?" He confirms, then asks, "What's your schedule?"

I stare at him, suddenly feeling slightly apprehensive about going to his domain. Even though I'm willing and just agreed to, I haven't given any thought to the details of an arrangement.

He smirks again, and damn, he's too cute. He leads me with his train of thought. "I'm assuming you're off tonight and that you weren't here to pick up a stranger. Therefore, aren't prepared to go back to your place? My place would be better."

He pauses, then adds. "Bella Rayne, this won't work if you don't trust me."

I sigh and nod. He's right. I don't want to go home alone, and if I can spend the rest of the evening in his arms... "Your place is fine."

We continue walking across the parking lot arm in arm, and he adds, "Remember two things whenever you're not sure. One, I'm a Navy SEAL. Two, I'm not him."

Seven

Jayden

At my Harley, I tell her. "This is my ride."

She nods, smiling. "I'm over there." She points toward a group of cars. "Where do you live?"

I tell her my address, and she fumbles in her pocket for her phone. "Hang on. I won't remember it."

"Just ride with me." I reach for the back

helmet, pull it to my chest, and unlatch the strap. "Time to start living again, Bella Rayne."

When I step up to put the helmet on her head, she takes a deep breath, closes her eyes, and braces for the helmet. I feel a pang of something I'm not accustomed to wanting. I want her to be happy. I want to be the one who makes her happy. I want to be the someone that restores her joy in living. Some sick bastard stole it from her.

Staring down at her beauty accentuated under the harsh lights of the bar parking lot, the sharp contrast of her dark arched brows and long thick black lashes against her pale skin, a strong urge to kiss her comes over me.

I move the helmet behind my back, prop it on my ass, sling my free arm over her shoulder and jerk her body to my chest. She lands hard on my chest, and I stare down into breathtakingly pure sapphire blue irises. A shocked gasp escapes her heart-shaped lips as her eyes spring wide open.

"Damn, you are fucking gorgeous," I whisper, then I steal whatever response she was going to say right off her face. My mouth devours her for a quick moment; then I set her free.

She gasps again, and before she recovers, I ease the helmet down onto her head. Latching the strap under her chin, those true-blue eyes twinkle like stars.

"Have you ridden before?"

"Not bikes. Horses."

"Not much different," I tell her as I swing my leg over and mount my machine. Then I push it off its kickstand and offer my hand to help her climb on. But she doesn't need me. She steps on the footrest, puts her hands on my shoulders, and swings her leg over. Then she settles her weight in the saddle like a pro.

When I crank it, it roars to life, and she wraps her arms around my waist. I don't worry about her balance when I put it in gear. I rev up the engine, and she squeezes me with her knees. She's an experienced cowgirl. Popping the clutch, jumping out of the parking spot, we tear out of the lot. Speeding down the highway, weaving in and out of the traffic, she lets out a 100% Texan cowgirl, "Yeehaw!"

My apartment is only a couple of miles from the bar, but she's enjoying herself so much I decide to take her for a long drive down the coast. The feeling of her hugging up tight behind me as we scream down the highway gives me an inner peace, I didn't know I needed.

When we reach the ocean, I pull over and park. Without needing my help, she swings her leg over and dismounts. As I rock the motorcycle onto the kickstand, she lifts the helmet off, shakes her thick hair out, and says, "Wow! That was exhilarating!"

I grin at her. "I thought you might enjoy a ride to the beach."

She latches the strap on the helmet, hands it to me after I've dismounted, then walks to the edge of the asphalt and waits.

"Have you seen the ocean at night?" I ask her as I join her.

"Honestly, I've never been to the beach." She says, staring at the ocean.

"What?" I stop and look down at her. "How long have you lived in San Diego?"

She cuts her eyes at me, embarrassed. "A few years."

"And you've never been to the beach?"

"Nope. This is my first time."

"Well, come on. Let me show you what you've been missing."

We enter the pier's walkway, and as we stroll to the end, she looks at me with an unreadable expression. "Do you love the ocean?"

"I do. Do you swim?"

"Yes, can we swim now?"

"Not here. This is a fishing pier. There are sharks in the water."

"Oh!"

"But we can go to a different beach tomorrow and swim."

"I thought being your Frog Hog meant only sex," she says as she hooks my arm and pulls it into her chest. Her firm tits hug it, and my cock thanks her.

"Don't worry. There will be plenty of that as well."

At the end of the pier, she puts her arms on the railing, leaning out as far as she can, looking down. "The waves are hypnotic."

"They are. Now, look up."

She does and gasps. "Dear lord! I haven't seen a sky lit that bright with billions of twinkling stars since Texas."

I step up behind her and wrap my arms around her so she can lean back and enjoy the moment.

She whispers, "Thank you."

"You're welcome

Eight

Bella Rayne

Heading back to the city, hugged up tight behind Jayden as we fly down the highway, I realize he is right. Age is a number that counts off years in a linear timeline, but that number doesn't define who you are inside. Right now, I feel sixteen and free.

When we arrive at his place, he whips through the parking lot, speeding down to the end, then brakes hard and stops. I dismount, remove my helmet, and he hands me his. I hold them watching as he pushes his Harley onto the sidewalk and secures it with a heavy chain to a black RAM 1500 TRX truck.

Then he opens the door to the apartment, and we go inside. He flips on the light, and we are standing in his living room. On this wall is a credenza with a television on top. On the opposite wall is his sofa with a coffee table, two end tables, and an armchair.

There is a Texas flag hanging on the wall over the couch. A runner rug is thrown on top of the carpet with tire impressions. He must park his Harley in here when he drives his truck.

The small single-person kitchen is in the back. There is a small dining area with a two-person dinette set and a small countertop.

He sets the helmets down on the credenza and asks, as he goes into the kitchen, "Do you want a beer?"

"No, thank you. I'll have water."

"Have a seat. Make yourself at home." He says as he gets the drinks from the refrigerator. "If you need to use the bathroom, it's easy to find." He points through the only interior door in the room.

"Thanks," I tell him as I head that way.

I pause in the bedroom doorway to find the light switch. Turning it on reveals a double bed, an end table, and a chest of drawers. Above the bed is another flag of Texas. The Gonzales, Come and Take It flag.

The bedspread is navy blue and made without a single wrinkle. The door to his walk-in closet is open but dark inside. I have no doubt it is as neat, clean, and organized as the rest of his apartment.

When I go into the bathroom, I find his toiletries aren't on his sink but in his shower. After I relieve my bladder, I join him in the living room.

"You're neat to be a bachelor." I tease him.

"Are you neat or messy?" He asks as he hands me the water bottle, already opened.

"Not nearly as neat as you are, but more neat then messy. I tend to scatter my stuff when I get home, then fall into bed exhausted. I clean up right before I leave the apartment that day."

"Do you make your bed?" He asks as he drinks his beer.

"Not every day. Somedays, I stay in all day."

He smirks.

I sit on the barstool and watch him work in his kitchen. He's efficient in his movements as he takes a pizza from the refrigerator, places it on a cookie sheet, and then pops it in the oven. He sets the timer, then asks, "Shall we sit on the comfy couch?"

I laugh, "Sure."

He holds his hand out for me as he comes around the counter, and before he sits, he sets our drinks on the coffee table. Then he pulls me onto his lap to snuggle.

The intimacy of being cradled in his strong arms gives me a feeling of comfort and security I haven't experienced since being a little girl. It's nice, and I relax as we talk.

"How long have you been a trauma nurse?"

"Four years. It's tough work, but it's rewarding. How long have you been a SEAL?"

"Years."

"Why did they call you FNG then?"

He chuckles, "I'm new to the team."

"What's it like being a SEAL?"

"I can't discuss it with you."

"Oh! I wasn't asking for mission secrets. I was just wondering what your life is like when you're not working."

"I sleep a lot." He laughs. "I live a pretty boring life."

I laugh too—"Same. I work a set schedule, but I don't imagine you do. What is your daily routine like?"

"If we aren't on a mission, we're training for one. Most of the time, it's between Monday through Friday unless it's for a specific mission. What is your schedule?"

"I work twelve-hour shifts, three days a week. Right now, I'm on Monday, Wednesday, and Friday."

The timer in the kitchen goes off, and he gives me a boost to help me get off his lap. We both go into the kitchen. He takes the pizza out, and I get us both a beer to drink with it. We sit at the little dinette table and exchange funny 'war' stories. I tell him about some of the absolute worse patients I have had, and he shares some funny training stories.

When the pizza is gone, we return to the sofa, turn on Netflix, snuggle, then crash.

Nine

Jayden

Bella Rayne stirs, then leaves the sofa. I reach out to grab her hand, "Where are you going?"

She whispers, "Bathroom. I'll be right back."

When her fingertips pull away, I sit up and stretch, shaking the cobwebs out of my head. I check my phone; it's 2:30 a.m. I clear the empty beer bottles off the coffee table, put them in the trash, and listen for the toilet to flush. When it does, I wait for her outside the door.

She turns the light off before she pulls the door open and takes three steps before I reach in and flip it back on.

The light floods the room and highlights her nakedness. She stops dead in her tracks. Her thick, soft brown curls hang like a curtain halfway down her back. Her skin glows in the light just like it did in the parking lot. The view steals my breath. Her perfect hourglass shape with her small waist, full curvy ass, and long legs as she spins slowly around turns every cell in my body on.

"Damn," escapes my mouth as her full plump breasts that sag slightly with their weight fills my eyes. As my gaze travels down her abs, where I placed my kisses in the stairwell, to her neatly trimmed pussy to her voluptuous hips perfect for gripping and fucking 'til she screams my name, my cock strains against my jeans, and I wish like hell I would have taken them off already.

She reaches her hand out to me as she backs toward the bed, and I swear my knees nearly fail me. In two strides, I'm on her. She braces for impact, expecting me to knock her backward onto the bed, but I stop, pulling up short to tower over her, to show my control, to demonstrate I'm dominant, yet my willingness to please her.

I drop my hips to hover inches away and bury my face in her neck. Inhaling her sweet scent, a low growl exhales with it.

Her head falls back, her back arches pushing her tits to me, and she breathes my name, "Jayden, make me yours."

The primal surge evoked is like nothing I have ever experienced before. My entire body reaches for her as my knees bend and my arms encircle her. She goes limp in my embrace, giving herself to me, and my mouth latches onto the first thing it touches. I suck so hard, wanting to devour her; I mark her. Her hands reach for me, claws out, and they dig into my back, scratching through my shirt. The pain feels oddly pleasing, and my balls draw up, causing my cock to thump.

Her fingers pull at the fabric as my mouth mauls her breasts, sucking hard everywhere, marking everything. The wildness she stokes within me feels dangerous and delicious. Like I was made to own her, and she belongs to me.

I ease her down onto the bed, then stand and

rip my shirt off. Staring down at her wanton look, I unzip my jeans and unleash my beast. A full-on hard-on springs out. The skin is stretched tight. The veins are already bulging, and how I'm not going to cum the moment I enter her is the only thought in my head as I push my jeans off and step out of them.

She raises her body onto her elbow to watch me strip. When I stand before her, just before I raise my knee to crawl onto the bed with her, she says, "that'll do it."

The off-handed compliment breaks my focus just enough to ease the danger of dumping my load upon contact, and I gain control again.

As I mount the bed, she holds her position and inhales, smelling me. She exhales a moan that sends me back into the danger zone. I place an arm behind her back, push her down with my chest, and then lift her weight and slide her body into the middle of the bed. I part her legs with my knee, and she spreads them for me. Without any more foreplay, I sink my cock into her. Our mouths moan in unison with the ecstasy.

As I thrust into her, building my speed into a frenzy, I can feel her pussy constricting and contracting with multiple orgasms. When I explode into her, her legs quiver uncontrollably as her eyes roll back into her head and her mouth forms into a perfect "O" shape.

I collapse onto her, breathing hard with the exertion, sweat pouring off me, and she whispers, "Mission accomplished."

After catching my breath and wits, I roll off her and pull her in tight to snuggle. She lays her head on my bicep, kisses my chest, and throws an arm and leg over me. Peaceful sleep seizes us both.

Ten

Bella Rayne

When I open my eyes, I find Jayden wearing a plush white robe and holding two cups of coffee. "I didn't know if you drank it black or with cream and sugar, so I brought both."

I stretch, happy and content for the first time in so many years I can't even remember the last time. Then I sit up and take the black one.

"Thank you," I tell him as my eyes devour his beautiful face. He gives me that cute permanent smirk that I'm 100% positive has gotten him out of a lot of jams and into even more.

"Aiden sent a text that there's a beach volleyball game." He states, and I'm sure he's telling me because he has to go, but unsure if I'm invited or not.

I nod and sip my coffee, waiting to see what my day will be like. Spent admiring this young man and absorbing all I can of the happiness being in his life gives me, or dreaming about him in my bed, resting up and counting down the hours until we are together again.

He says, "I'll catch a quick shower, and then we'll go to your place."

I nod and point to the coffee cup he's still holding. He grins, "Both?"

I nod again, and he sets it on the nightstand for me and then leans in for a butterfly kiss. I pucker up, and he places a sweet little peck on my lips. I know I look a mess, but his eyes tell me I'm beautiful.

As I drink the caffeine and become coherent, I look around the room. He's picked up his clothes, and mine are folded neatly on the chest of drawers. He's left the door to the bathroom cracked, and I see him moving around inside.

Then I hear the shower running, and he disappears.

Thinking I had ten minutes, or more was a mistake. In less than five, the water stops, and he steps back into view.

I gulp the remaining coffee down, jump out of bed and into my t-shirt, skipping my bra to save time, and wiggle into my jeans. Then I hurry with the two coffee cups into the kitchen, rinse them out quickly because Jayden's place is sterile, and I respect that in a man, even though I'm not.

Then I grab my phone to check the time. It's nearly noon.

He appears in the doorway of the bedroom, stark naked. My heart seizes and then starts thumping hard in my chest. To see his magnificence on display in broad daylight is impressive as hell. His neck is thick and strong. His shoulders are broad and curved like bowling balls. His pecs are pronounced: thick, strong, and expansive. His waist isn't trim, but it's small. His abs are washboard perfection. Forget Jell-O shots. Whiskey shots could be drunk from them. The "V" between his hips points to a cock that is the epitome of perfection. Its flaccid state speaks to its size and ability. His legs are straight, thick, and muscular.

"Damn!" I say and cover my gaping mouth. "You are fucking fine, young Jedi."

He chuckles, holds his hand out for me to take, and says, "Damn, you're dressed."

Drawn to him like a magnet, I walk over and place my hand in his. He pulls me to him and puts his arms around me. I wrap him in a hug, wishing I hadn't been so stupid as to put on my clothes now. A quickie before I go would be nice.

He kisses the top of my head and says, "I'll be right back."

I follow him into the bedroom to watch him, admiring his body without the pretense of modesty. He opens a drawer, removes a pair of swim trunks, then sweeps my bra off the top to fall into it, closing it.

I smirk as he steps into his swimsuit, "I guess I won't be needing that."

He grins and winks, then walks into his closet. Curious, I follow him and lean against the door frame. It is exactly what I thought. Neat, clean, and organized, but crammed full of shit. From winter coats to suits to casual dress shirts, slacks, jeans, stacks of tennis shoes, and boots. His complete wardrobe is in here.

He pulls a tank top off a hanger and puts it on.

Leaning in the back corner is a bag of golf clubs with a tennis racket stuffed inside, a slalom water ski, a snowboard, and a surfboard.

He removes the surfboard and says, "If the waves are good, I can show off for you."

I grin, relieved I'm going and excited he would want to impress me.

Then he slips on a pair of flipflops, and I follow him to the door. He takes his keys off a hanging hook on the wall and says, "We'll take the truck."

I wait in the truck with his surfboard and three empty coolers as he unchains his Harley, pushes it inside his apartment, and locks it up.

When he's behind the wheel, he nods to his phone, "Enter your digits and cue up your address."

I take it and do as he's instructed, but laugh and tease him, "You either don't trust me to give you good directions, or you don't trust yourself to remember how to find me. Which is it?"

He smirks, "Neither. I won't have your

address so I can surprise you with flowers because our weekend together has been amazing."

"Oh!" I stare out at the road, floored by this romantic man.

He cuts his eyes at me, "You seem surprised by that."

"I am." I turn in the seat to look at him.

But before I can say anything, he says, "Remember, number two? Apply it."

Eleven

Jayden

It takes us fifteen minutes with the Sunday traffic to travel five miles. When we arrive, I'm surprised to discover she lives in an upscale gated community. When I turn in, I lower the window. The guard walks out looking like he's walking forward with his pants on backward. Bella Rayne leans down and says, "Hey, Garrett."

"Hey, BR, who's this? Your little brother?"

I give him my best player smirk but don't say a word.

Bella Rayne stays serious and professional, ignoring his baiting, "Garrett, I told you. I don't have any family."

He nods his head at me. "Then who is he to you?"

I bite my tongue, clamping down on 'boy toy, buddy,' trying to escape.

She ignores him, "He's allowed to come and go without me. I'll forward his information to the office."

He bows as if given a command, backs away, and opens the gate.

"Don't say it," she says as we pull through.

"Say what?" I tease her. "That the dude is into you?"

She shakes her head. "He's the manager's nephew, and he's just for show. The cameras work on facial recognition and license plates. I live in 2A."

When we pull up to her parking spot, she explains, "I saved the life of the owner's mother. Otherwise, I could not have afforded the rent."

"Good for you. It's nice."

"Come on in and make yourself at home. I don't take a shower as quickly as you do."

As soon as we enter, she starts picking up her things and straightening the room. "There's water in the fridge if you want and leftover Chinese food." She points to the kitchen.

"Water sounds good. I thought we would grab lunch at a food truck on the boardwalk at the beach."

"That sounds good." She calls over her shoulder as she walks through her bedroom, heading to the bathroom.

She lives in a fully furnished two-bedroom, two-bath apartment. I walk into her kitchen and retrieve a water. Then walk around examining the little knickknacks she's personalized her home with while I hydrate.

She has an abundance of horse statues made of porcelain, glass, and carved wood. I smile, knowing how good she would rock a flannel shirt tied under her tits, with her abs exposed over a pair of hip-hugging too short jean shorts, a big ass Texas state belt buckle, a pair of cowboy boots, and a cowboy hat.

When I enter her bedroom, I see one framed

photo on her nightstand and realize there aren't any other family photos. I walk over to the bed, set the water bottle down, and pick up the picture.

It's of her when she was a teenager. She's holding the reins of a white horse with one hand. The other is under his head, and an older teenage boy is standing on the other side. They are posed for the camera and smiling. I set it back down and walk into the bathroom.

"Who's the boy in the picture?" I ask her.

She answers over the running water. "Oh, that's my brother, Enrique."

I look over my shoulder at it. "He doesn't look anything like you."

"He's my foster brother."

Hmm. That's interesting.

"And the horse?"

"That's Smokey. He's my baby."

I smile. She's a horse girl then. No wonder I was attracted to her. Horse girls are empathic, good communicators, and love unconditionally.

"How old were you then?"

"Fourteen, I think." She slides the shower door open and reaches for the towel. I grab it first and dangle it for her.

The cold air draws her tits into tight little

buttons, and goosebumps pop out. "Come here. I'll dry you off."

She looks down at the tile floor, and I realize she could bust her ass if she does, so I wrap her up and carry her to the bed.

Setting her next to it, I tell her. "This is going to be a problem today."

"What?" She says as she wraps the towel around her body and walks over to her dresser.

"This." I laugh, and she looks back. My cock is clearly outlined against my swim trunks.

She laughs, "So much for staying frosty."

"I need your help with this before we go." I walk up behind her and wrap my arms around her, opening the towel and cupping her breasts.

Twelve

Bella Rayne

By the time we are on the road again, heading for the beach, we are both starving. After he stops by the grocery store and fills the coolers with bottles of Budweiser and ice, he whips in an In-N-Out Burger so we can eat on the way.

Wishing for a Whataburger instead, we chat about growing up in Texas, reminiscing about the little things that made it special. From the lightning bugs on hot summer nights to eating tacos for breakfast to the number of rides we went on at Six Flags Over Texas.

I discover he grew up riding horses too, and I tell him about Smokey. How he saved my life. His hand opens for mine while I share briefly losing my parents, entering the foster care system, and being saved by Enrique and Smokey at the Equine Therapy Ranch. The gesture is just one of the many little things I realize he does to express his tender side. He shares that he's never lost a family member and comes from a big family.

When we pull up, he tells me again how beautiful I am, places a peck on my lips, then enters a world I've never experienced.

We get out of the truck and are mobbed by his SEAL 'brothers' and their families. All of them fussing about the beer truck being late. The men grab the coolers, Jayden grabs his surfboard, and I'm grabbed and hugged by Cindy Braswell and the other wives. All of them talking at once.

"Do you have sunscreen?"

"So, you've landed our Luke."

"Where are you from?"

"Where do you work?"

"Do you have kids?"

"Here, put on my hat. Do you need a pair of sunglasses?"

I do my best to answer them all.

They have set up a volleyball net on the beach and several umbrellas. My day is spent cheering for my man, laughing at my man, waving to my man, and kissing my man. All while being surrounded by friends who are family.

At the end of the day, as the sun sets, Jayden and I say goodbye to the last couple. We've decided to stay and watch the sunset. As they drive away and we walk back down through the sand to our donated beach towel, Jayden asks, "Remember, number one?"

"I do."

He smiles and sits, opening his legs, and putting me between them, hugging me from behind. Watching the gorgeous yellow ball turn pink, then red, and sink into its mirrored reflection, we don't speak at all. We enjoy the moment and the magic.

It's late when we return to *Suds After BUD/S* to retrieve my car. He parks the truck behind it, blocking it in, and tells me, "I had an amazing day today."

I smile, "Maybe so, but it wasn't as amazing as the day I had."

He grins and leans over for a goodnight kiss. As soon as his tongue touches mine, a sense of wanting to belong to him, to wanting this to be the first day of the rest of my life, comes over me. I pull away as panic fills me.

His soft, "Hey, don't," sends me fleeing from the truck. Before I can get my car door open, though, he is pinning me to it. His hands in my hair, holding my mouth still, forcing me to be his. His kiss isn't harsh. It's soft, soothing, and calming. My breath syncs with his, and I give him what he wants—all of me.

Tears flow down my face, and he wipes them away. "Number one and number two."

I try to grin but can't. "It's not that," I manage to say. "It's this." I throw my arms around him, pull him to me, and kiss the ever-loving fuck out of his mouth.

He gives better than he receives, and if we weren't in a public place with cameras, I'm sure we would be fucking right now.

When he lets me go, he whispers on my lips. "Don't be afraid of this." Then he pulls away, runs his thumb over my lips, and says, "I'll follow you home."

"Stay with me," I beg him. "I don't want this night to end."

His smirk isn't cocky. It's everything.

Thirteen

Jayden

Her alarm goes off, and I open my eyes. She tries to untangle herself from me, but I hold her in place. "Good morning, sunshine," I say over the alarm.

She laughs, "The sun isn't up."

I grin, rolling over and mounting her. "I wasn't talking about the orb in the sky that gives light. I was talking about the sun shining radiantly from you. The blue is gone."

She grins and pecks my face. "Yes, it is. Thank you!"

"You're welcome," I tell her as I trace my fingers down her face. "Do we have time to start your day off right?"

She giggles, "No! I didn't get enough sleep as it is, and if there's an emergency today, I don't need to function on adrenaline."

She pushes me off and says, "Sleep in, and let yourself out."

I roll off, hug her pillow, and tell her, "Kiss me before you go, and you have to change that alarm. It's awful.'

She laughs as she turns it off. "That's why it's effective."

When she places a kiss on my cheek, she says, "Text me when you're up. I can't talk, but I can text."

Several hours later, my eyes finally opened. I look around the room, disoriented until I remember the beautiful, kind, sweet, funny, intelligent, easy-going cougar I've managed to make this incredible agreement with. I stretch, scratch my nuts, and lay staring up at the ceiling, reliving the remarkable day we spent together yesterday.

I've dated many girls, but I've never dated an older woman before. She is just the right amount of everything. No frivolous drama over her hair or nails. No makeup. She's appreciative of the little things and dedicated to her career.

I throw my arms into the air and shout, "YES!" Then I close my eyes and take a nap. Her shift is twelve hours, and I have nothing planned today but rest. Might as well rest in her nest.

It's nearly noon again when I finally roll over and check my phone. There are several texts from my team, all congratulating me on landing a woman like Bella Rayne. She fit into our family easily, but of course, she would. She's their age. I'm the one who's the duck out of water.

I send my woman a text.

Good morning, babe.
How's your day going?

She doesn't answer immediately, so I throw off the covers, sit up, and look around. The picture of her and her horse and foster brother catches my eye again, and I pick it up to examine it closer.

Her hair was shorter and darker than she

wears it now. The freckles that dot her nose are already there. The intense focus in her eyes is also present at this age. Her smile lights up her face. She looks happy in the picture, but I know this was a tough time for her. I smirk, another testament to the strength of her character.

I set the picture back on the nightstand. I don't know who the bastard is that stole her sunshine, but if I ever meet him, I'm going to introduce him to my knuckle sandwich and kick his ass properly, collecting at least two of his teeth. I'll hand his ass to him on a silver platter.

Bullying bastard. He stole her youth from her, but he didn't break her spirit.

She answers my text.

IS IT STILL MORNING?
OH, YEAH, IT IS.
IT'S BEEN BUSY.
WE'VE ADMITTED ONE.
ARE YOU STILL AT MY PLACE?

YES, I'M STILL NAKED IN YOUR BED. DREAMING ABOUT YOU. LOOKING FORWARD TO TONIGHT.

AH! THAT VISUAL.
YOU LOOK LIKE AN ANGEL
WHEN YOU'RE ASLEEP
BUT YOU SNORE
LIKE THE DEVIL.
LOL! I HAD TO FIND
MY EARPLUGS.

LMAO! SORRY ABOUT
THE ZZZZS. COULDN'T HELP IT.
I WAS EXHAUSTED. SOME HOT
PIECE OF ASS WORE ME OUT.
GOOD THINKING ON
THE EARPLUGS.

She doesn't respond, so I wander into the kitchen after using the bathroom. She has made a pot of coffee, but it's cold. I find a cup and heat it in her microwave. Then open her refrigerator and look for something to eat. It's bare compared to mine, so I decide to grab a shower and head to the diner I noticed yesterday to eat breakfast.

I smile as I slurp my coffee on the way to the bathroom. If they have tacos, I'll order them and send her a picture. Breakfast tacos are the best.

I'm in the shower when she texts.

> SORRY ABOUT THAT.
> WHAT ARE YOU DOING NOW?

I wrap the towel around my waist and snap a picture for her.

> AH! THANK YOU!
> YOU AREN'T A FIGMENT
> OF MY IMAGINATION AND
> I HAVEN'T BEEN DREAMING.
> I HAVE BRUISES ON MY ARM
> WHERE I PINCHED
> MYSELF YESTERDAY.
> LOL. FOR REAL.

I chuckle at that.

> I'LL HAVE TO KISS
> THOSE SPOTS TO
> MAKE THEM BETTER.

> *FRANTICALLY PINCHING MYSELF
> FROM HEAD TO TOE NOW.

I laugh out loud with that visual.

WHAT ARE YOUR
PLANS TOMORROW?
I WOULD LIKE TO SPEND
THE DAY WITH YOU AGAIN.
*PRAYING YOU WANT TO
SPEND IT WITH ME TOO.

> I SPEND THURSDAYS
> WITH SMOKEY AT
> CATALINA RANCH.
> WOULD YOU LIKE
> TO JOIN US?

What? I look at the picture on the nightstand.

THE SAME SMOKEY
IN THE PICTURE?

> YEPPERS.
> HE'S MY BABY.
> I CAN CALL AHEAD AND
> GET A HORSE FOR YOU.
> YOU DO RIDE, DON'T YOU?

OF COURSE!

Texan, remember?

Yee-haw!
Gotta go. Car crash.
Kisses!
...Everywhere.

As I lock up, my phone rings. It's Catalina Ranch confirming they have a two-horse trailer we can rent. I smile as I climb into my truck. She's going to absolutely love this surprise.

As I approach the exit gate, I see Garrett having a heated discussion with a man in a car. I spool my window down and lean out to get a better look and feel for what's happening. I recognize the man from the bar the other night—the one who sat next to Bella Rayne.

Garrett: "You're not on the approved visitor list. I'm not opening the gate for you."

I wave at Garrett, "Yo, man, is there a problem? You need some help?"

They both look at me. The dude in the car seems surprised to see me, but he covers it quickly and smiles. "No, no problem."

Garrett turns to face me. "I'll open the gate for you as soon as he leaves."

I nod and wave that's acceptable but stare down the man in the car. He puts the vehicle in reverse and backs out.

When Garrett opens the gate, I pull through and ask, "I thought I recognized him. Was he trying to get in to see Bella Rayne?"

"No, he asked if an Allison Girard was living here. I told him, 'no,' but he wanted to enter and look for her car. Said he was an uncle. Obviously, that's not allowed."

"You did a good job, Garrett. Handled it very professionally."

He smiles, "Thanks."

Fourteen

Bella Rayne

When I arrive home from work, I toss my keys on the counter and go straight to the refrigerator. Taking the Chinese leftovers out and munching them, cold, right out of the box, I pour myself a glass of white wine.

I'm exhausted. The car crash had four critically injured, and we were non-stop for five straight hours trying to save lives. I stayed late to help the second shift too. When I finally got out of there, everyone was alive and stable.

Jayden sent a text around six, offering a hot meal and a bottle of my favorite adult beverage, asking if I wanted to crash at his place. But I turned him down. I'm just too tired. I need sleep, not sex, or I will be an absolute zombie tomorrow.

When I enter my bedroom, I discover Jayden made my bed before he left and laid out a button-down the front shirt and a pair of cutoff distressed jean shorts. He rolled the bottom of the shirt up and tied the ends together. I cock my eyebrow at that. My tits will seriously be in danger of blackening my eyes. My cowboy hat sits on top of my Tony Llama brown leather boots.

There's a handwritten note on top.

> Bella Rayne,
>
> Please wear this sexy cowgirl outfit for me. (Notice there isn't a bra or panties.)
> I have a day trip planned I think you're really going to enjoy. I'll pick you up at eight.
>
> Jayden

After a nice hot, long shower, I dry off. Wrapping my wet hair in a towel, I pull back the sheets to climb in and text him. Sitting on my pillow is another handwritten note.

> I left a kiss on your pillow.
>
> Sweet dreams.
>
> Your Jedi

I place my lips on it and smooch. Then I roll onto my back and send him a text.

ARE YOU STILL AWAKE?

He doesn't answer right back, and my eyelids are heavy.

Thank you for the kiss.
I'll see you in the morning.
Your cowgirl, Frog Hog.

When my alarm goes off in the morning, I laugh, remembering Jayden grumbling about it yesterday. I throw my covers off, excited to spend the day with him no matter where we go or what we do.

While the coffee is brewing, I jump back under the water to wet my hair. Going to bed with wet hair is not a good idea.

When Jayden arrives at eight, I'm standing on my porch waiting for him, dressed in the clothes he set out for me to wear.

When I climb into his truck, he lets out a long catcall whistle, and I give him the biggest, brightest smile I possess. He leans over for a kiss, and I hold my cowboy hat in place as I smooch a wet one on his lips.

"Yeehaw, cowgirl. You look sexy as fuck!" He grins at me as I settle in the seat and strap my seatbelt on. It rests against my bare braless cleavage and misses the thin cotton fabric of my shirt, which splays open, giving him an eyeful of my tit.

"Where are we going?" I ask him, pretending the look on his face isn't making me wet and horny.

"It's a surprise." He says as he pulls down to the gate, and it opens automatically for him. He lifts a finger wave to Garrett, who gives him a nod.

"Does that mean no hints?" I ask as he pulls onto the road, and his GPS gives him directions to Catalina Ranch.

"Affirmative."

"Grrr," I growl, making him laugh.

"So, tell me, what's yours and Smokey's history?"

As we drive, and I open up about my past, sharing with him how Smokey saved my life, he listens. I omit a lot of the little details, just hitting the highlights.

My parents died. I was placed in foster care. Equine therapy. Being assigned Smokey. Working a job to buy him.

When I'm done, he asks, "Did you come to California for college and bring him with you?"

I hesitate but then tell him. "No, I was in an abusive relationship and ran away. I rode him here."

His eyes widen, shocked by my answer, "Are you fucking kidding me?"

"Nope. I was eighteen and scared. I knew I would be killed or worse if I didn't flee."

He looks at me. "My mind is blown."

"It only took us about ten days. It wasn't that big a deal." I laugh. "When I arrived, I found Catalina Ranch, boarded Smokey, worked odd jobs, got my nursing degree, and love my life."

"Have you been back?"

"To Texas?" I look at him like he's grown two heads to even suggest it. "No, it's best for me to stay away. He won't have forgotten. He's pure evil and would punish me before killing me or ..." I say 'the worst' aloud. "Sell me as a sex slave."

"Sounds like the kind of man we pursue and eliminate."

I laugh, "Why do you think I chose San Diego, the home of the Navy SEALs?"

He grins, "So, I don't have to remind you of number one, I'm a SEAL, or number two, I'm not him?"

I shake my head. "No, that's the only reason we met."

When we arrive at the ranch, I direct Jayden to Smokey's stall. When we turn down his aisle, I'm surprised to find him tied to a two-horse trailer and a bay horse. Jonny greets us and then guides Jayden as he backs his truck up to hitch to the trailer.

"Where are we going?" I can't hold the question anymore.

Jayden grins as he tosses the two saddles into the back of his truck while Jonny loads and secures the horses. "Ever heard of Norco?"

"Are you shitting me?" I ask.

"No, I thought we would have lunch and explore the town."

"Oh my gosh! Jayden, this is the best date EVER!"

An hour and a half later, we arrive, unload the horses, saddle them, and ride into Horsetown, USA. We spend the entire day riding through the town, hitching the horses to the posts provided when we want to go inside and eat or just window shop. We also ride some of the trails. It was the best date EVER!

On the ride home, he gets a call from Aiden.

The look on his face sends my heart into palpitations. This side of the Jedi is the serious warrior. He tells his team leader, "Roger that. 0500. Out here." Then he looks at me and breaks the news. "We're being spun up."

I shake my head. "I don't know what that means, but I assume it means you have a mission?"

"Yeah. That's all I can tell you too."

I'm surprised that he doesn't share more, but I shouldn't have been. SEALs are the elite of the best, and Jayden is part of the elite's elite. I learned from the other girlfriends and wives at the beach that they are Tier One special warfare operators, and Jayden is the youngest in over a decade to make the team. When I asked for clarification, they said, "SEAL Team 6."

My jaw dropped. "That's the team that took out Bin Laden."

Cindy Braswell nodded. "None of our men were part of it then, but yeah, that's the team they are on."

"Wow," I looked out at the men playing a competitive volleyball game and felt honored to be there.

Fifteen

Two weeks later ...

Jayden

When I dropped Bella Rayne off at her apartment, I didn't intend to go inside. But she untied her shirt, took it off in the doorway, and then backed inside. Like a moth to the flame, I followed her in.

Two hours later, I left her.

The jet touches down, and we're back on American soil. Grabbing our gear, the team unloads, and heads to our cages. It was a successful capture, and my SEAL Team 6 mission cherry has been busted. No more FNG buys beer for everything. Aiden opens the door to our area and asks, "You heading to Bella Rayne's?"

I grin at him, "Straight away."

He laughs. "Oh, boys," he announces to the team, "Our little Jedi is in love with the cougar!"

Snarls, growls, roars, meows, and hisses erupt, then they all purr, and it's funny as hell. I tell them, "Yeah, yeah." But grin, knowing it's true.

When we were working, I was honed in on the mission, tuning out all the noise and emotion of the outside world. My training kicked in. Focused and sharp.

But as soon as it was over. Bella Rayne was on my mind.

Clothes changed, gear packed away, personal items in my pockets, phone and keys in my hand, I head to my Harley and Frog Hog. My heart aches to crush her tight to it, needing to sync with hers. My lips long to kiss, nibble, and taste her.

To nuzzle her neck and smell her. My cock yearns to coax my name from her lips.

As soon as my phone powers up, text messages fill my inbox. I scan the senders looking for the only one that matters. The first few days, she sent updates, like diary entries. They are amazing to read.

> Hey, Jayden. Hope you're alright and the mission is going well. I'm back to my old routine of work, work, work, sleep, sleep, sleep. The only difference is my nights are filled with dreams of you and my days are filled missing you. Oh, and I kiss my pillow every night before I fall asleep. And I changed my alarm. I now wake up to Seal Team Navy fitness cadence. Can't wait for you to hear it.

Okay. Out here.
See what I did there ;)

Hey, Jayden
Day two of missing you.
It's occurred to me you probably don't have your phone so there's no need for me to look at mine every hour on the hour, but I do anyway. Because what if you return and I don't know it! So as soon as you do, please send me a text and let me know. I can't wait to kiss your lips again.
Your Frog Hog.

Hey, Jayden
Day three of missing you.
I spent the day with Smokey. It was good to get away and ride. The weather has been nice.

> I think I'll drive
> to the beach later
> and stare at the stars.
> I miss you more than
> I want to admit.
> I'm afraid I'm not
> holding up my end
> of our agreement.
> You know that whole
> tough talk about
> not having a full-fledge
> romantic relationship with
> commitment and expectations?
> I think I might
> dig that after all.
> Missing you this terribly
> means something, right?
> Dare I sign off,
> Love,
> Bella Rayne?

But then they stopped. Nothing. Nothing!

I call her, but she doesn't answer. Her voicemail does. Since she hasn't recorded a personalized message, I don't bother to listen to the robotic voice. If she checks her phone, she'll see I've called and will call me back.

I hang up as a dread so deep in my soul it hurts comes over me. Something has happened, and no matter what it is, it isn't good. I pull my helmet onto my head, buckle the chin strap, push it off its kickstand, and crank the bike. When I pop the clutch, I pop a wheelie. Then scream out of the parking lot like the hell hounds are after me. Racing to Bella Rayne's apartment, my training kicks in, and I seize control of the ice in my veins.

When I pull up to the gate, I snatch the helmet off so the camera can recognize me. It's after four, so Garrett isn't on duty. The gate slides away, and as soon as the gap is big enough, I tear through it.

Her car isn't parked in her spot, but I stop to check if she is home anyway. When I try the door, it's locked. I bang on it and her bedroom window, calling her name, but nothing. Nothing!

I mount my bike again, and when I'm through the gate, I head straight for the hospital. I don't park. I stop in the emergency lane and ask the security guard on duty when he comes over to tell me I can't park there. "Listen, I'm looking for a trauma nurse. Do you know Bella Rayne Parker?"

"Yes," he says. "I know Bella Rayne."

"Is she here?"

"No. Is something wrong?"

"I'm not sure. I've been out of town and just got back. But she's gone dark. I can't find her, and she's not answering her phone."

He lifts an eyebrow, "Who are you?"

"I'm her boyfriend," I tell him.

"You think maybe she might be ghosting you?"

I shake my head. "Not a chance in hell."

He believes me and says, "She hasn't been to work in over a week. I thought she had finally taken a vacation."

The dread in my gut tightens as I crank my bike again.

He tells me over the noise. "I hope you find her."

"I'll find her."

When I scream out of the parking lot and hit the highway, I head straight for *Suds After BUD/S* bar.

Sixteen

Somewhere on the outskirts of
Tijuana, Baja California
Mexico

Bella Rayne

STANDING IN FRONT OF THE WINDOW, I watch the sunrise. Today must be the day Manny arrives. I can't wait to see him. The bile rises in my throat, and I practice gathering enough saliva now that I'm semi-hydrated to spit it in his face.

Last night, I was taken out of the cage I had been held in for at least five days. I have no idea how long I was unconscious from the time they took me to the time they brought me here.

I sigh as the memory of Jayden's beautiful face passes randomly across my thoughts. I've realized it shows up when I'm close to breaking. I shake the tears away.

The two men hosed the filth off me, laughing at how I spun around, trying to ease the pain from being blasted with a pressure nozzle. Then my hands were bound behind my back and attached to the rope tied around my ankles. My skin is raw today, where the wet rope chafed it.

Because I refused to walk, I was slapped repeatedly in the face. I'm sure they were told not to leave bruises, but I'm pretty certain my left cheek is turning blue. It's tender as hell.

They stuffed me in the trunk of a car and drove down a graveled path, took a highway for less than a minute, then turned onto the concrete driveway of Manny's mansion.

Entering from the rear of the house, I was taken by two women who showed no emotions about what they were doing. Stoic and stone-faced, they gave me a proper bath with warm water, soap, shampoo, and conditioner.

Still tied and bound, but by decorative cord now, I was put into a room off the kitchen and spoon-fed broth on the hour every hour for five hours. Then I was given a bottle of water and drank the whole thing without taking a breath.

Told to rest, I was placed in this room. It's sterile, holding only a cot. I shuffle back to it, lie down, and close my eyes. Not because I want to sleep, but because I don't want to think or feel.

When the door opens, it's thrown wide and bounces off the wall. I sense his evil enter before I'm snatched up and forced to face him. Staring at the devil can be unnerving, but hatred is a powerful drug.

I collect my salvia and wait. When his hand grips my throat to imprison my will, I spit it in his face.

He lets out a blood-curdling laugh that would curl the hair of Mother Mary herself. Then he releases me, and I stand my ground, defiant.

He wipes his face with a handkerchief he pulls from the inside pocket of his black suit before he says in a low menacing tone meant to intimidate me. "You are going to be punished for that."

"So be it." I smile at him.

"Sassy as ever, I see."

"Always."

"We shall see how long that lasts." He states then he turns on his heel and marches out.

I hobble to the door and slam it as hard as my bound body can fling it. The sound echoes in the sterile room.

His evil laugh travels through it, and I start to shake.

Immediately, a woman enters the room and tisk-tisk's me. "Now, you listen to me." She shakes her fingers at me. "If you want to live, you need to adjust your attitude. Right now! 'Cause, that evil bastard won't hesitate to slit your throat, and I don't want to have to clean up after your rebellious ass. It's pointless, but it's not hopeless."

My mouth goes dry as a vision of Jayden's face floats by, and I hear his words whispered in my ear. "Remember two things whenever you're not sure. One, I'm a Navy SEAL. Two, I'm not him."

I close my eyes and feel the tears falling off my face as I nod. "I understand. I do want to live."

"Good!" She says as she holds out a pill. "Take this. It'll help."

"What is it?" I ask as I take it and place it on my tongue. "I'm a nurse."

She smiles, "It's Special K."

"Ketamine," I nod, thankful for the assistance that isn't habit forming.

"If you're cooperative and obedient, you won't be given heroin. He doesn't like to waste it on his girls."

I nod, "Thanks."

"I'm just doing my job so I can survive. He wants you naked, so I don't have anything further to do until he's ready for you."

"Do you know when that will be?"

She shakes her head. "No idea. You're a special case. He flew in just for you."

"Do you know how they found me?"

She shakes her head. "Even if I did, I wouldn't tell you. I don't want my tongue cut out."

Seventeen

Jayden

I hit the elevator button to the bar but can't stand still and wait for it to arrive. I stride over to the stairwell and pull the door open. The memory of fucking her in here hits me right between the eyes, and the reality that I may never see her again —alive, sucker punches the wind out of my gut.

As I take the stairs three at a time, the exertion calms my chaos. When I emerge, I stride straight to the bar, lean over it, and look for Mick. He's at the other end, but he sees me and gives me a head nod. I hang my head and breathe steady deep breaths while I wait for him.

"Sup, young Jedi? You guys make it back tonight?"

I ask, "When was the last time you saw Bella Raync?"

His head jerks to the side, instantly concerned. "The last time was when you two left together. Why?"

"I can't find her. My gut tells me she's in trouble."

"What makes you think that?"

Suddenly the dude that hit on her that night pops into my head, and I see him arguing with Garrett the next day.

"FUCK!" I look around as it dawns on me, he knew her and was stalking her.

"What?" Mick asks. His law enforcement training kicking in.

"The dude that sat next to her that night. Have you seen him again?"

"No. He got really uncomfortable when he realized the bar was full of SEALs. It happens more times than you might think. You guys are an intimidating bunch."

"He showed up at her apartment complex the next day, but she lives in a gated community, and the security guard wouldn't let him in. I didn't put two and two together because he was asking about a woman named..." I replay the conversation I had with Garrett, "Allison Girard. He wanted to know if a woman named Allison Girard lived there."

"You think she's Bella Rayne?"

I nod. "I do now. Damn it!" I tap the bar with my knuckles. Thinking about what my next step should be.

I need to speak to Garrett. Find out if the man came back. Get his tag number from the security camera. Probably stolen, though.

Mick says, "She shivered when she mentioned an evil ex that night." He covers my hand with his and stops the tapping. "Come with me. Crockett is in his office."

I shake my head. "I need to go back to her place and ...."

Mick says, "Crockett hunts traffickers. Come on."

I follow him to a side door. He knocks, then

turns the handle and pushes it open. "Rocket, this man needs your help."

I can see Crockett sitting behind a desk. He immediately stands and waves us inside. Mick introduces us, and as we shake hands, Mick explains what he knows so far. Crockett motions for me to sit, but I can't.

He listens to Mick, then asks, "How long have you known her?"

I cringe, "Long enough to know she didn't go willingly."

Mick says, "She's been a regular here for a couple of years. Always on a weeknight, keeps to herself, doesn't get drunk, leaves alone." He looks at me, and I see the pain in his eyes. He knows how bad this is. "The young Jedi here has been the only person she's flirted with."

Crockett's frown says it all. "She's one of ours then."

He looks at me with steel in his eyes. "Sit. I need to make some phone calls."

Mick turns to me and offers his hand. "Don't worry. You're going to get her back." Then he says, "Sit down."

I watch him walk out, listening to Crockett on the phone with someone named Foxtrot. He pauses and says, "Jayden, go pour us a drink. Then sit."

I look at him, and he nods to a table on the opposite wall where a crystal liquor bottle sits with four matching glasses. As I walk over, he turns on a smart TV mounted on the wall. I glance at it as I pour two glasses.

A beautiful woman stares at me. "Jayden, my name is Nina Foxx. I'm Crockett's wife and the targeting officer of his company. We will find, rescue, and return her."

I nod as I hand Crockett a glass. He lifts it and waits until I do the same. Then we gulp the contents down. The fire in my throat feels good, and the warmth when it hits my stomach calms my nerves. I sit as Nina explains what they do.

"Our company is called Coq Blockers. Our team consists of former SEALs who continue to protect and serve our country. Our mission statement is 'freedom is not an option.' Sit tight and let us do what we do."

I nod, "Yes, ma'am."

"First question. Do you have a picture of her?"

"I do." I pull my phone out and flip to one I snapped when we were at the beach.

"Give it to Rocket."

I slide my phone to him, and he scans it with his.

"What's her name?"

I answer, "Bella Rayne Parker, but I believe that's an alias."

She nods. "R, a, i, n?"

"No. R, a, y, n, e."

"What do you believe her real name is?"

"Allison Girard from El Paso, Texas."

She nods, "I'll get back to that. How old is she?'

"Thirty-two, I think."

"Where does she live?"

I give her the address, and as she fills in a profile of Bella Rayne, Crockett is typing on his laptop. He slides my phone back to me.

"The team is assembling at our base in Vegas."

Eighteen

Bella Rayne

I STARE UP AT THE CEILING, WATCHING AN array of colors swirling around Jayden's face. I know I'm hallucinating from the Ketamine, but as long as Jayden appears, I embrace it, knowing it won't be a bad trip.

When the effects wear off, I close my eyes and sleep.

Hours later, the woman who came in earlier

returns. "He's ready for you now." She holds another pill.

I shake my head. "No, thank you."

She says, "It's not optional. Either take it willingly, or I'll call for help and shoot it straight in your veins."

I swallow the pill, knowing I don't have a choice and pray Jayden's dream returns.

She leads me on a leash down the hall, weaving through corridors to get to his suite. By the time we reach Manny, I'm floating in colors, dancing with my Jedi.

When I waltz in, he laughs, "I see your mood is better."

"I see you're old as fuck now." The woman jerks my leash, and I fall to my knees.

He snorts, "I have the power to bring you to your knees and make you beg."

I laugh at him and point, "Your puny penis never satisfied me."

The woman jerks my leash again, and I look at her. She's frowning, upset with me, but her eyes ... I travel inside them ... are laughing. I burst out laughing with her. "Now, that was fucking funny!"

She pushes me out, and I lay on the floor staring up at the ceiling, giggling.

He walks over and slaps her. "What did you give her?"

She bows her head, afraid, "Special K. Same as the others."

He glares at me. "Why isn't she cowering then."

She shrugs, "She's not afraid."

He grunts and snatches me up by my hair. But it's cut too short, and he can't get a handful big enough to hold my weight. I stick my tongue out at him and blow. My spit dances out of my mouth and then turns to daggers and stab him. I roar with laughter, and he drops me.

The kick he delivers to my gut flips a switch. I move like a ninja, sweeping his feet out from under him so effectively, that his heavy frame keels over backward and crashes to the floor. His head bounces off the floor twice, and his eyes roll back in his head.

The woman gasps and screams, then she stops herself, scared of drawing attention. "Is he dead?"

I snatch my leash out of her hand. "Not yet."

It turns into a snake and winds around his

neck, hissing. Tighter and tighter, it winds itself —until the woman unhooks me from it, grabs my hand, locks the door behind us, and runs with me back down the corridors to the area where her quarters are.

When we are behind the door in her room, she says, "Dios mío! ¡Dios mío!" She looks around her room, finds a summer dress my size, and shoves it at me. "Pon eso."

My hallucinations are over, and I stare at her. "What the fuck just happened?"

"Pon eso." She points to the dress. "Put that on. HURRY!"

I slip into the dress, and she zips up the back for me. Then points to a pair of flats, "Wear those. We have to get out of here. You killed him."

"I did what?" I stare at her, gobsmacked.

"You killed the devil." She grabs me and hugs me tight. "Por amor a todo lo que es santo. We have to get out of here."

She grabs my hand again and leads me further into the house. When we hear voices, she hides us in a room until they have passed. Then we go into an extensive library with a tile floor and randomly scattered tables. She heads straight for one in the rear corner, pushes a secret button on the inside leg, and I smile as a hidden door slides open.

Of course, there would be an escape route.

We hurry down the stairs, and she flips the switch on the wall of a mining shaft-like corridor, and it seals itself shut. Once it's in place, I take my shoe and bang the switch until it's broken.

We race down the tunnel together. At the second junction, we stop. She tells me, "When you emerge, leave the trees. There are cameras. Walk with the mountains on your left. Good luck, ángel."

She pushes me into the tunnel I'm to take, then runs into another. I sprint, and jog, then sprint again. I stay straight at the next two junctions. When I see a house door at the end, I stop to catch my breath. Then I ease up on it and listen, putting my ear against it. It could be a door that leads into a restaurant or a house. I reach out and turn the handle, easing the door open.

What I see, makes me cry. The desert splayed out before me. The house door hangs on the side of a mountain.

Nineteen

Jayden

Four hours later, we know what happened. Bella Rayne left her apartment and was followed by a black SUV. She stopped for a red light, and it pulled alongside her. She was the lone car at the intersection. Two men jumped out of the back, while another jumped out of the passenger side. They executed a perfect snatch and grab. One of them drove her car to the hospital and parked it in the extended visitor parking lot. Then he walked inside and vanished. The vehicle carrying her drove straight to a stash house on the lower side of San Diego. They carried her inside, stuffed in a duffle bag.

Two days later, they moved her. They cut her hair short, dressed her like a fat man, and marched her out. They crossed the Mexican border in a ratty, old Cadillac, drove through Tijuana, and traveled south for twenty minutes. She was held inside a small house on a Mexican cartel's compound until this morning.

This morning, they moved her to the mansion on the hill. Two hours later, which is around the time our team landed from our op, the head of the cartel, The Diablo Gang, Manny Morales, arrived.

I check my G-shock watch. The Coq Blockers team should be at the Mexican border by now. The plan is to cross on horseback, infiltrate the mansion, and steal her back.

Standing next to Crockett and Mick in his office, we watch the mission unfold on the smart TV. It's split into two monitors. One is the live camera on Mike Franks' helmet. He's running the mission. There are five other men with him. The other is the live camera on the overwatch drone. Nina's voice calls the action, but it's operated by someone they call License to Own.

Franks comes over the com. "HAVOC, this is One. We're ready for go."

Nina answers, "Copy One. You are clear for go."

Franks answers, "Good copy." Then he says to his team, "Execute."

For the next hour, there is radio silence as they ride into Mexico and thread their way through the terrain past Tijuana, heading for the Diablo Gang compound.

Then Nina breaks the silence. "One, this is HAVOC. Stand by."

"Copy HAVOC. Standing by."

Nina says on the monitor. "Rocket, do you see that?"

"I do."

She asks, "License, can you zoom in on the tango moving north?"

The infrared camera zooms to a magnification close enough to identify the white spot moving north across the scorching desert in the middle of nowhere is a woman.

I hold my breath.

Nina says, "Switch to the HD camera and let's identify who that is."

The screen goes dark, then the most beautiful woman in a soft brown cotton shift comes into focus.

Nina lets out a "BINGO!"

The breath I was holding escapes as relief washes over me. She's alive. She's escaped. But she's not out of danger yet.

Nina cues up the team and gives them the good news and the GPS coordinates.

The screen switches back to infrared and zooms wide enough to display the team moving to their target.

As they make their way to Bella Rayne, she walks north at a steady pace. She turns around periodically, observing the landscape.

When she spots them, she stops walking and starts waving both hands over her head.

Franks cues the mic. "Target insight."

Franks' camera captures the moment. He identifies himself, but she doesn't make small talk. She asks, "Who's my ride out of here?"

He chuckles and points to a man who rides his horse up to her. The man speaks, but we can't hear what is said. He laughs, then leans down and braces in the saddle. Bella Rayn grabs his arm, and he lifts her off the ground. She swings her leg over the horse, hooks it, and pulls herself up behind him.

Crockett tells me. "That's Jack 'Hammer' Black. He's also from Texas."

Everyone is laughing when she grabs the saddle and settles in. Then they turn around and ride home.

When they cross the border, Franks says, "Mission success."

"Good copy," Nina answers.

Twenty

Jayden

An hour after the rescue...

I'm on my bike following Crockett to the airport. He had a helicopter waiting for her at the border. Now that she's safe, the emotions start to infiltrate my training. I don't know what I will say to her, but the last 24 hours have been hell! I might never have seen her again if it weren't for Jeff Crockett and the Coq Blockers team.

He drives his black SUV around the airport to a private hangar, and I park next to him. He puts his arm around my shoulders as we walk inside. "We haven't discussed money." He says, and I cut my eyes at him, knowing I'll gladly work the rest of my life if I have to.

A distinguished-looking blonde man in a dark suit walks across the hangar towards us, and Crockett says, "That's because this guy makes that a nonissue."

They hold their hands out to shake, and Crockett says, "Hardcore, I'd like you to meet Jayden Evans. Jedi, this is Aurelius Moore. The CFO of Coq Blockers."

I hold my hand out and pump his, "Thank you!"

He smiles and says, "You're welcome. They are three minutes out." He turns, and we walk to the tarmac. He and Crockett make small talk while I brace myself for the onslaught of emotions I'm about to experience.

I know I agreed not to have a romantic relationship. That we would stay frosty, but she said in her text that she wants more now, and that was before all this went down. I smirk. I suppose it's safe to confess that ship sailed for me in the stairwell.

Being on the receiving end of a victorious rescue mission's homecoming is a humbling experience. Watching the aircraft approach, knowing who's inside, the anticipation for the physical reunion is intense but pales compared to the feeling of karma that draws two souls together.

As soon as the helo sets down, I'm running to it, and as soon as the door slides open, she bails out, running to me. Jumping into my arms, wrapping her legs into a full-body hug, I feel complete again. It's going to be mighty tough to beat the happiness of this moment.

Epilogue

Bella Rayne

Two weeks after the rescue...

I STAND JUST INSIDE THE DOORWAY IN Crockett's office, shaking like a leaf. I still can't believe everything that has happened to me. I pinch my arm, and Cindy hugs my neck.

"Stop that. This is really about to happen."

I roll my eyes and try to say something, but I'm speechless. Then the knock on the door sends my heart racing out of my chest.

Before she opens it, she looks at me and says, "You look radiant." Then she slips through it, and I count to thirty just like we rehearsed.

I take a deep breath and open the door. Standing at the end of the aisle formed by the people who love and support us is the man I'm about to marry.

His sexy as fuck smirk plastered on his handsome as hell young face reassures me that I'm not dreaming. This is really happening. I have found not only the love of my life but been given a second chance to live my life freely.

As I slowly walk down to the beat of the traditional wedding march, I have eyes only for Jayden. When I stop, he offers his arm, and we walk up together onto the stage and exchange our wedding vows.

The whole thing doesn't take ten minutes, but it's the best ten minutes of my life. When the justice of the peace pronounces us husband and wife, Jayden cups my face between his hands and thrusts his tongue down my throat.

The roar of "HOOYAH" drowns out the band playing.

Then we turn to face our friends, who are family, and begin our lives as one.

Thank you for reading TARGET BELLA.
I hope you loved Bella Rayne and Jayden's story and will leave a review for others.
Direct link to Amazon Review page:
https://readerlinks.com/l/3626809

Continue reading Jocko Malone's romance:
Coming Home For Her
https://readerlinks.com/l/3356666

"Fabulous! Great love story. Well written!" - Kindle Customer

In high school, the unassuming Jorja Jones became the unlikely target of the 100mph fastball star, Jocko Malone. To her, his 'Juicy' nickname was bullying. To him, he was flirting.

When he joins the Navy instead of going Pro,

unwilling to leave without seeing her again, not knowing if he would return or not, and unable to speak with the raw emotion stuck in his throat, he pinned her against the lockers and took a goodbye kiss then walked away—detonating her world.

Now, six years later, when Jorja receives an assignment to write an article on Everyday Heroes for Modern Family Magazine, she is thrilled with the honor—until she learns it's on Sunnyville's newly returned hero, Navy SEAL Jocko Malone.

When past and present collide, the explosion destroys all Jorja's beliefs about the young cocky, arrogant ass she remembered. As she learns who he really is and what he is all about, assessing him in a new light as he interacts with his K9 partner, she fights not to fall for the hero he has become.

Can she accept her feelings for him before he walks away forever?

"This is now my favorite book by Jessika Klide!" - *Kindle Customer*

"What a truly inspiring and heartfelt story. I teared up so many times. This made me proud to be an American." - Goodreads review

PROLOGUE

Jorja

I slam my locker door, spin the lock, and freeze.

"Sup, Juicy?" Jocko Malone leans down to laugh in my ear.

Trying to ignore him but knowing he won't let me; I roll my eyes as I close them and grit my teeth. "Stop calling me that!"

"Why? You and I both know it's true." He croons, making my knees weak.

I bite my tongue because he's right. The minute I catch a whiff of his musky scent, my panties are wet, and it pisses me off that I can't control the way my body reacts to him. Jocko is too arrogant and too cocky because he's too gorgeous, but I refuse to fawn over his perfect ass like all the other girls. It's disgusting the way they prostrate themselves, wanting his attention. I have more self-respect than that and self-discipline.

Defiant, I stand, slinging my backpack over my shoulder in a pitiful attempt to knock him away.

He laughs harder, then whispers in my ear. "You are going to have to do better than that to make me back off."

"Gawd, you are so infuriating! Why do you torture me?"

"Because I can ... and because you are so damn delicious when you get all pissed off."

I start to push him away but think better about it. If my pussy soaks itself with his scent, how will it betray me if I touch him? No .... I don't need to make that mistake. "Move, Jerk-off. I'm going to be late for class."

He laughs out loud at my feistiness, enjoying my resistance way too much, but he steps back.

Without another word, I stomp off.

Margie giggles when I walk up. "Jocko teasing you again?"

I grit my teeth and nod my head.

She giggles harder. "Honestly, Jorja, I don't know what your problem is. If Jocko Malone were flirting with me like that, I would be in heaven!"

I roll my eyes at her. "You don't know him like I do."

She snorts. "What's there to know? He is 6'4" and glorious!"

"He's an ass!"

"So?" She shrugs. "He's a 6'4" glorious ass!"

I shake my head. "Come on. We don't want to be late for class."

Jocko

Watching Jorja stomp away is nearly as good as staring down her shirt at her tits when she kneels at her locker. Her body's built like a brick house, and her anger adds a twitch to her stride that jerks her booty from side to side.

"Hey, Jocko," Britney says as she slinks in to

take Jorja's place. Her eyes glued to me like I'm her next meal.

I open my locker but keep an eye on her. She's pinched my ass and grabbed my junk before.

She steps closer. "So, is it true you throw a 100-mile-an-hour fastball?"

I shut my locker and give her a look that means 'I don't have time for your stupid games,' but she doesn't take the hint. She knows it's true and had her response already planned.

"Oh," she says, so breathy it's more like a moan.

Mrs. Strickland's voice comes over the intercom. "Jocko Malone, please come to the office."

Britney giggles wickedly. "What did you do this time?"

I ignore her and walk off, but she's hot on my heels. Following like a puppy, it pisses me off. I do an about-face and crush her hopes face to face. "Barbara, don't follow me."

"My name isn't Barbara."

"Whatever. You are fucking ugly. Do not follow me."

My mother would roll over in her grave if she

knew how I talk to these girls but being crude is the only thing that makes them back the fuck off.

She glances around to see if anyone overheard, then she slinks away.

The sad part is she'll be back. She'll gang up with her friends, and they'll talk about what a shit I am. They'll give her a makeover, and she'll try again.

I push open the office door. Mrs. Strickland greets me with a smile, "Jocko, take a seat. Principal Davis wants to have a word with you."

Parking my jeep at Sunnyville High, I head inside. It's been a week since graduation, and already I feel out of place. Walking through the hall, the atmosphere is relaxed. Everyone's milling around, waiting for the bell to ring.

When I round the corner to the lockers, I see Jorja. Her back's to me, and her long hair hangs straight down. She's leaning on my old locker laughing with Margie.

I'm going to miss teasing Juicy.

Joseph Pruitt walks up to her. His smile and his posture piss me off.

He's hitting on her.

When she smiles at him, a vise clamps down on my heart.

When he hands her his phone, an unknown force punches the wind out of my gut.

When she begins to tap the device, giving him her digits, realization hits me right between the eyes, and I advance on them.

Margie's face lights up when she sees me, then her mouth drops open, and her eyes bug out of her face.

Both Jorja and Joseph turn to see what's frightened her.

My eyes lock on Joseph's, and he starts stuttering. "Jocko, I … I thought y … you were gone."

I grip his shoulder, and he visibly cringes, then I hand shuck his stupid ass away. "Backoff, Motherfucker." I growl.

He stumbles, slips, lands on his ass, then crawls away.

When I turn to face Jorja, Margie takes a few steps back, clearing the space between us.

Jorja's eyes narrow, and she opens her mouth to say something sassy, but her words are lost.

I'm on her. Pushing her body against the locker, I pin her there with my own.

She stiffens in resistance, and her eyes flash with anger, then defiance.

But this time, I don't taunt or tease her. This time, I cup her face and tilt her lips to take my kiss.

As I lower my mouth to hers, the defiance in her eyes fades to fear as her willing body melts into mine.

Damn. I've been a fool. I should've done this a long time ago. She's been resisting me, not because she doesn't want me, but because she does.

My lips crush hers, and a blast of sensations overwhelm me.

The sweetness of her scent, the softness of her breath, the exquisiteness of her essence fills my emptiness completely. I press her willing body, needing to feel her curves meld into mine. Then her lips part and her mouth opens, wanting my tongue.

All the years of hunger and longing for her bursts forth, and I devour her like a starving man. Every sensation shoots through me like lightning, and I can't get enough of her.

When I finally release her mouth, silence

surrounds us as I stare into her eyes, burning this moment into my brain, knowing this may be the only time I hold her in my arms.

My throat tightens with the raw emotion of saying goodbye, making my words impossible to express. But I want her to know. Holding her face captive, I stare into her eyes, trying to bare my soul to her.

Jorja Jones, you have always been the only one I have wanted, and when I come home ... if I make it home, I want to come home to you.

The bell rings.

I set her free, hoping her heart will wait for my return.

Then I turn and walk away to become the man I am meant to be.

A SEAL in the US Navy.

CHAPTER ONE

Jocko

"Welcome to Sunnyville." I read the sign at the city limits. "We made it, Luce. The first stop is my parent's gravesite. I need to pay my respects."

Driving down the road, I chat about losing them. "The days after the accident were dark. I was so angry. Most people don't know this, but I would sneak into the graveyard to sleep with them under the stars. It sounds morbid when I say it out loud, but it helped."

I hit the blinker and slow down to make the turn into Sunnyville Crematory and Mortuary. "I know they would be proud of the man I have become. Did I tell you I could have played pro baseball? No? Well, I could have, but I decided my life needed to matter more than making people cheer. I haven't regretted my decision either. Not for one day."

Parking, I pick up the bouquet of flowers for my mom and open the truck door.

"Come on. I want my parents to meet who is responsible for my safe return home."

Turning down Willow Bend Street, I wonder out loud. "We are going to swing by Juicy Jorja's old house and see what's up. Is she going to be the one that got away? Or is she waiting for me to return?"

As I cruise by her family's old house, she gets out of a car parked in the driveway. I hit the brakes and slow down as I hone in on her in full stalker mode. The first thing I notice is her hair is short, shoulder-length, cut in layers, and bounces as she walks. The second thing I notice is her body is still built like a brick house. All woman. All curves. Instantly, that old feeling only she was ever able to conjure rises out of my groin.

Watching her bound up the steps two at a time to unlock the front door tells me she still lives there.

I notice several additional interesting things as well.

There are no toys in her yard. Therefore, she isn't a mom.

There are a couple of small signs in the yard. An advertisement for a lawn care service and a warning that her house is protected by a security system. Therefore, she lives alone.

There is a For Rent sign on the house next door. Therefore, she needs a new neighbor.

I grin in the rearview mirror. "Looks like we have found a place to live."

———

Rounding the corner off Willow Bend Street, I tell my boy, "Next stop, Aunt Betsy, and Chief's house. Now, listen, if Moose is still alive, go easy on the old dog."

"Waah. Waah." Two short sirens pop off, and I glance in the rearview mirror to see a cop car tailing us.

"Well, shit." I pull over on the side of the road and put my window down. "Stay calm, Luce."

I lay my pistol on the dash in clear view and dutifully put my hands on the steering wheel in plain sight.

The officer walks up and sees the handgun. "You got a permit for that?"

"Yes, sir."

"Anyone sitting back there?" He leans in to look in the back.

"My dog."

"License, registration, insurance, and carry permit, please."

"They're in the glove box."

The officer takes a step back, puts his hand on his weapon, and instructs, "Reach slowly and get them out. Keep your hands where I can see them at all times."

Just then, another cop car pulls up, and Grant Malone, my first cousin, gets out. "What the fuck, man? Are you kidding me?" He strides over with no regard to the other officer, but tells him as he passes, "Lou, this is my cousin, the Navy SEAL, Jocko Malone."

Office Lou takes a step back, so I unlatch my seat belt and exit the truck.

"Welcome home, Cuz!" Grant wraps me up in a big bro hug, slapping me hard on the back.

"Thanks, man. It's good to be back."

Nate, Grant's partner, walks around the front of their cruiser. "Well, I'll be damned." His outstretched hand clasps mine. "Welcome home, Jocko."

Officer Lou offers his hand. "Nice to meet you. I have heard a lot of things about you."

"Likewise. All good, I hope."

"You just getting into town?" Grant beams. "You should have told us you were coming."

"Naw, I like having the element of surprise on my side."

They laugh.

"I hope you're heading to Mom and Dad's. She'll be upset if she isn't your first stop."

"Taking my boy to meet them now."

Grant's eyes light up. "You got a boy?" He walks over to the back door and opens it, then takes a step back.

Sitting on the edge of the seat, ears forward and alert, eyes focused and drilling Officer Lou (who he smelled fear from), totally ignoring Grant (who's a big dog lover) is my solid black Belgian Malinois K9.

"Oh ... he's a good-looking son of bitch. What's his name?"

"Luce."

My boy cuts his eyes at me.

"Isn't that a girl's name?" Grant teases.

"He's confident in his masculinity." I chuckle. "It's short for Lucifer."

They all laugh, and Nate says, "That suits him!"

I snap my fingers, and Lucifer jumps down and heels.

Officer Lou takes a step back. "Is he safe?"

"For the most part." I tease him.

I reach down and ruffle Lucifer's hair. "He's my boy. He's my good boy."

Lucifer's tongue rolls out and dangles. One ear twists to the side, and I swear, he laughs.

"Pet or K9?" Nate asks.

"Retired with distinction, so pet now. He's an MPC, multi-purpose canine. He does it all. I'm hoping we can hire his skills out once in a while. Part-time, emergency gigs. He tracks, sniffs bombs, drugs, and he's badass at takedowns."

"Good to know." Grant says, "I'll pass that along to Chief Ramos. I'm sure the community can use his skills on occasion."

"Appreciate it. He gets bored when he isn't working."

"I'm sure Emerson would love a part-time jumper if you're down for doing it."

"Absolutely!"

Their radios squawk as a call comes in. Nate responds as Grant sticks his hand out. "I'm sure Mom will put together a welcome home party for you. We'll catch up then."

I shake it. "You bet."

I offer my hand to Nate. "Nice to see you again."

And to Officer Lou. "Nice to meet you. We done here?"

He grins. "Yeah, you're good to go."

I look down at Lucifer. "Let's go meet your Aunt Betsy, Chief, and cousin, Moose. We don't want to get on her bad side."

Grant must have called Aunt Betsy and given her a heads up that I was on my way over. She and Chief are standing on the porch when we pull up, beaming with pride.

For the next hour, we sit on the back deck, watching the dogs play in the yard and catching up. Lucifer runs laps around and around Moose, who is content to let him.

I share with Aunt Betsy and Chief as much as I'm allowed to say about our missions. Which is very few actual details, but what I can share sounds really cool to civilians.

"How long is your visit?" Chief asks.

"I'm home for good."

"Oh, my, that makes this old woman very happy!" Aunt Betsy gets up to give me another hug.

Chief offers, "You're welcome to stay here while you settle in."

"Thanks, but I have already booked a place at The Cottage, and I saw a house on the way in that's for rent. I'm going to check into it. It would be perfect."

They exchange a look. "It wouldn't happen to be on Willow Bend Street, would it?"

A lopsided grin slides sheepishly across my face. "Maybe."

"I certainly hope so." Aunt Betsy smiles.

I stand. "Listen, I have taken up enough of your time today, but I wanted to make sure I stopped by on my way in. I learned a lot over the past six years, and one thing is how important family is."

When I push open the office door at Bruins Realty, Lucifer's on a leash.

"May I help you?" The receptionist asks.

"I'm here to rent the house on Willow Bend Street."

She looks at her computer screen and

informs me, "That house's listed with Maxine Reynolds. May I have your name?"

"Jocko Malone."

She types. "Maxine will be right out to help you."

She doesn't bother hiding her curiosity and looks me up and down. That old feeling of about to be groped returns, so I take a seat on the couch while I wait.

"He's a beautiful dog. What's his name?"

"Thank you. Luce." I look down, and he leans his head over and rubs my leg affectionally.

"Normally, we don't allow animals inside."

"Good thing he is't an animal. Good thing he's very well behaved."

She smirks.

Maxine walks in all smiles. "Jocko Malone?" She offers her hand, and I stand to shake it. "Maxine Reynolds. I understand you want to see the house on Willow Bend Street?"

I shake my head. "No, ma'am. I want to *rent* the house on Willow Bend Street."

"Well, that makes my job easy. Right this way then."

Walking over to Sunnyville Trust and Loan, Lucifer and I pass Fire Station 13.

Suddenly, I hear, "Jocko?"

Grady Malone walks toward me with a huge grin on his face. He wraps me up in a big bro hug. "Cuz, it's good to see you."

"Good to be home."

"And who do we have here?"

"Luce."

Grady rubs his head and cuts his eyes at me.

"Lucifer." I laugh.

He chuckles, rubbing his head and scratching behind his ears.

"He served five of the six years with me. Saved my life more than once. He's kinda special."

Grady ruffles his neck, talking doggy goo-goo to him, but in a manly way. "He's a good boy. A real hero."

"Yes, he is."

"Mom called and told me you were home. She's already planning a welcome home dinner for you."

Just then, the firehouse lights strobe, and the alarm goes off.

Grady reacts instantly, grabs my hand,

pumps it once, "Glad you're home. Can't wait to introduce you to Dylan."

"Looking forward to connecting again."

He runs inside, and I look down at Lucifer. "Come on, Luce. We don't want to get run over."

―――

When we walk in Sunnyville Trust and Loan, everyone stops and stares. A man comes out of a side office and walks over with his hand outstretched, "Jocko Malone, I presume?"

"One and the same."

"The whole town is already talking about your return. What can Sunnyville Trust and Loan do for you?"

"I'd like to open an account and transfer my funds."

"I can take care of that for you. Right this way." He escorts me into his office.

"News travels fast." I comment on the way as people continue to stare.

He chuckles. "Maxine called."

―――

An hour later, Lucifer and I are heading to Miner's Airfield to see Grayson. After my parents passed, Aunt Betsy made sure her three boys were always around, so I didn't feel totally alone. Of course, they turned spending time with me into a competition. But Grayson had the advantage. He had Luke.

When I pull up to Mercy-Life, he's standing outside, grinning from ear to ear, dressed in his flight suit with two helmets in his hand. The first words out of his mouth when I step out is, "Airborne in five?"

"Abso-fucking-lutely!" Opening the back door, Lucifer jumps out and heels instantly. "Let me grab his flight gear."

He springs into the bed of the truck, sniffs through the bags, bites the one holding his gear, lifts it, and brings it to me. I unzip it and pull out his jump vest, goggles, and ear protection. "Yes, you're going." I tell him, and his tail wags.

Walking back to Grayson, he starts prancing, excited to be doing something more than lounging around.

"I take it he likes to fly?"

"He likes to work, and since we have been transitioning out of the military, we haven't been able to do much of anything but run. I'm looking forward to getting settled and getting us both back in shape." I bend down and strap his gear on.

Grayson scratches his cheek, smirking. "Cuz, if you're out of shape ..." He eyes me up and down, then says, "Do the Malone brothers a favor for old times' sake? Don't challenge us in front of the wives."

I laugh. "Don't poke the bear then."

"Fair enough."

On the way to the helicopter, he asks, "You settling down in Sunnyville?"

"Yeah, I have unfinished business here."

"Her name wouldn't happen to be Jorja Jones, would it?"

I grin. "It would."

Continue reading:
Coming Home For Her
https://readerlinks.com/l/3356666

Coq Blockers Security Team

Jeff Crockett, aka Rocket
Target Nina
Chief Executive Officer (CEO)
Mission Team Leader
Former Navy SEAL Tier One
Special Warfare Operator
Alpha 1
Height: 6'5"
Weight: 260

Maximus Aurelius Moore, aka Hardcore
Mr. Sexy in 9G
Chief Financial Officer (CFO)

Billionaire Investor
Former Army Aviator
Apache and Blackhawk Pilot
Height: 6'0"
Weight: 200 lbs

Nina Fox, aka Foxtrot
Target Nina
Chief Operating Officer (COO)
Mission Team Commander
Former Tier One Targeting Officer
For Alpha Team

Meghan Meadows, aka Ambassador
Chief Liaison Officer (CLO)
Mission Coordination Team Member
Former Army ISA Officer

Mike Franks, aka Mr. Mom
Mission Team Member
Former Navy SEAL Tier One
Special Warfare Operator
Alpha 2
Height: 6'0"
Weight: 200 lbs

Jack Black, aka Hammer
Target Logan
Mission Team Member
Former Navy SEAL Tier One
Special Warfare Operator
Alpha 3
Height: 6'1"
Weight: 230

Jocko Malone, aka Fastball
Coming Home For Her
Mission Team Member
Special Warfare Operator
Former Navy SEAL Tier One
Special Warfare Operator
Alpha K9 handler
Height: 6'4"
Weight: 250

Lucifer, aka Luce
Coming Home For Her
Mission Team Member
Special Warfare Operator
Former Navy SEAL
Belgian Malinois

Multipurpose K9

Brody Andrews, aka Badass
Target Lizzy
Mission Team Member
Special Warfare Operator
Former Navy SEAL Tier Two
Special Warfare Operator
Height: 6'3"
Weight: 265 lbs

Justin Davis, aka Danger
Moving Back For Her
Mission Team Member
Former Marine
Height: 6'3"
Weight: 230

Zane Lockhart, aka Insane
Making Good For Her
Mission Team Member
Special Warfare Operator
Former Navy SEAL Tier Two
Special Warfare Operator
Deputy Sheriff - K9 handler

Height: 6'1"
Weight: 210

Batman, aka Bruce Wayne
Making Good For Her
Mission Team Member
Law Enforcement
Belgian Malinois
Multipurpose K9

Dirk Sam, aka Sam-I-Am
Manning Up For Her
Mission Air Support Team Member
Former Army Aviator
Apache and Blackhawk Pilot
Height: 6'2"
Weight: 225

Micah Young, aka Dark Thirty
Mission Technical Support Team Member
CIA Agent - Hacker

License To Own
Mission Team Overwatch
Drone Operator

Civilian Video Gamer

Nikolai Smirnov, aka Grappler
Opening Up For Her
Mission Team Hand-to-Hand Combat Trainer
Former MMA Champion Fighter
Height: 5'10"
Weight: 185

Jessika writing as Stingray23
HOT Military Romantic Suspense

A Few Good Men

Target Lizzy

Target Nina

Target Logan

Target Marie

Target Bella

Jessika writing as Cindee Bartholomew

The Liotine Heir

American Flyboy

Italy's Most Eligible Bachelor

Worth The Risk Series

Secret Life

Stunning Secret

Shocking Secret

Dark Secret

Twisted Secret

Startling Secret

Standalone

Twisted To Get Her

Read Jessika's newest, sexiest, and most talked about bestsellers...

LIFE IN LIVE OAK

Coming Home For Her

Moving Back For Her

Manning Up For Her

Opening Up For Her

Making Good For Her

SUCH A BOSS

Big Book Boss

Big Booze Boss

BILLION HEIR

Fraudulent Fiancee

Escaping in Glass Slippers

Accidental Amnesia

THE HARDCORE NOVELS:

SPECIAL EDITIONS

Untouchable Billionaire

Unstoppable Billionaire

Unforgettable Billionaire

THE HARDCORE COLLECTION:

TRILOGY BOXSETS

Undeniable Chemistry

Unbridled Passion

Unwavering Devotion

THE HARDCORE SERIES:

ORIGINAL SIRI'S SAGA

Mr. Sexy in 9G

The Cock-Tail Party

The Perfect Man

It's Ladies Night

The Battle is On

The Sex Pot

In Heaven at Last

A Shakeup Occurs

He's Hard Core

The End of Her

A Shakedown Happens

Family First Always

Learn more at

JessikaKlide.com

Stingray23

Top 4 Amazon Chart author of HOT romcoms Jessika Klide's alter ego, Stingray23 pens HOT Military Romantic Suspense Thrillers.

#4 Amazon Chart Author of HOT billionaire romance brings her readers the perfect blend of heat, humor, and heart.

JOIN JESSIKA'S VIP READER'S LIST
for exclusive giveaways, new release information, sales, and more.
https://jessikaklide.com/

Newsletters not your thing?
No worries.
— CONNECT ON SOCIAL MEDIA —

- goodreads.com
- facebook.com/JessikaKlideRomance
- instagram.com/jessikaklideauthor
- bookbub.com/authors/jessika-klide
- x.com/JessikaKlide
- tiktok.com/@authorjessikaklide

Stingray23.com

JessikaKlide.com

Made in the USA
Columbia, SC
21 July 2024